Bridging gaps between poets

P | O | L

Poetry Out Loud

Short Stories | Prose Poems | Reviews

P | O | L
Issue : 04 | Year : 04 | July 2022

Advisory Board
David Lee Morgan
Gauranga Mohanta
Ashoke Kar

Editor in Chief
Uday Shankar Durjay

Associate Editor
Louise Whyburd

Section Editor
Sudip Chakroborthy

Managing Editor
Joseph Inhong Cho

Administrative Assistant
Sudip Bishwas
Anindita Mitra

Special Correspondent
Dayal Dutta

Jacket Design
Shan

Image Design
Abbie Neale

Publisher
S Pen Union London
E: poetryoutlouduk@gmail.com
Available at Amazon - Paper Back and Kindle
Price: £10 | $10 | €15 | Tk. 500 | Rs. 350

Contents

Part One
Author Profiles (15-40)

Part Two
Short Stories (43-105)

Part Three
Prose Poems (109-151)

Editorial

The first question that would come to the reader's mind is what is a short story? A story is a story but how do we recognise a short story in modern literature. The first thing there should be is a click which makes readers rethink and try to find the solution to an unsolved expression or conclusion. In a short story, there should be a single place instead of multiple places and one or two characters. Some other characteristic of a short story is a single plot. It can be read in one sitting and the length must be no longer than around 60 minutes. A short story is like every other type of essay writing but what is special about it? Straight away it should draw in the reader and capture their imagination. Anton Chekhov (1860-1904) a modern short story author realised and understood that life is godless, random, and absurd and that all history is the history of unintended consequences. He designed his stories to appear agonisingly, almost unbearably lifelike and he also represented the end of the first phase of the modern short stories.

A short story is a part of fictional writing in prose which is shorter than a novel. Edgar Allan Poe in his essay 'The Philosophy of Composition' expressed that a short story should be read in one sitting anywhere from a half-hour to two hours. It would be experimental and use an uncommon prose style and unusually narrate the emotion. In 1842, Edgar Allan Poe wrote in his review of Hawthorne's Twice-Told Tales that a skilful literary artist has constructed a tale. He also believed that the definitive characteristic of the short story was its unity effect. Rabindranath Tagore has got an epic opinion regarding the short story- 'Tiny soul tiny pain tiny words / Very simple / Thousands of forgetfulness / floating every day / a few drops of tears / No description of the incidents / No theory no advice / It would be incompleteness in the heart'. The end is not the end. In the 21st century, the writer's diversity in thinking and imagination are wonderfully recognised in their created chronicles. From Ernest Hemingway's Big Two-Hearted River (1925) to Elizabeth McCraken's The Irish Wedding (2021), readers might find a lot of good examples of narratives in the contemporary short story era.

Prose poetry is another vital part of extant literature, I mean the latest fictional and nonfictional time. In 1990, Charles Simic won Pulitzer Prize for his prose poetry collection 'The World Doesn't End.' POL especially works for prose poetry; however, we have included a short story this time. After announcing the 4th issue of POL we received huge responses from all over the world. People are profoundly interested in short stories which have moved me significantly. I think the short story and the prose poetry are a good combination in the literature. Sometimes (not every time) we may find a slight difference between the short story and prose poem. Some short stories carry the sounds of prose poems like Margaret Atwood's Murder in the Dark, a collection of short fiction, published in 1983. Anyway, POL's aim is to try and come away from traditional poetry and create a vast platform for prose poetry writers. Behind this publication, we work very hard to leave a distinctive signature in contemporary literature. Gauranga Mohanto, David Lee Morgan, and Louise Whyburd have spent precious time and put in a lot of hard work to publish it. Editing is the biggest part to publish any kind of magazines or anthologies. I started in 2019 just with a little ambition and my dream is growing now as time goes by. We are grateful to the readers who have a keen interest to read the POL in their busy life. We tried our best to deliver a great piece of work and wish it would be continued further.

Part One

Author Bio

D. A. "Roarshock" Wilson is a San Francisco poet, author of First Hours of a Rainy Day and Other Poems and publisher of Roarshock Page, a literary street flier. He reads regularly, locally, and internationally, in person and via the social web, and can be found online at his website. www.roarshock.net

James Tian's works have been published in more than 50 newspapers and magazines in China and abroad and have been translated into many languages. In 2018, he was awarded the second prize in the national excellent literary works competition for the 15th anniversary of the resumption of the publication of *Jinggangshan* writers' daily and was awarded the special role model of The Times in 2018. Second prize in *Wen Yiduo* poetry competition in 2018; BPPW gold award in 2019; Award for excellence in Latin American literature in 2019; Award for American poetry in 2019; Bronze medal of "Bena" award for French poetry and song in 2019; In 2019, he won the silver award of the American Pegasus poetry award and other awards. The International Culture Publishing Company published the monograph "the light in the sky" *Tianyu* modern poetry anthology, Sichuan Nationalities Publishing House published "*Tianyu* lyrics anthology", China Ground Publishing House published "*Tianyu*lyrics anthology 2" and other books. He is the Representative of the art-literary Movement IMMAGINE & POESIA in China.

Fin Hall, the New Pitsligo-based poet and artistic organiser extraordinaire. Fin is the host of Like a blot

From The Blue, a poetry and spoken-word event transcending the boundaries of the physical and digital welcoming in hundreds of creatives from across the globe as well as a regular open mic night at The Blue Lamp Fin is a profoundly experienced poet with a career spanning decades. On-stage, Fin performs with a beautiful sensitivity. He isn't afraid to broach upon themes of old age, hope, love, and loss but reserves a potent and fiery attitude against injustice. Fin is also a filmmaker, collaborative writer, performance poet and this year, as well as adding a second regular venue for his Blot shows, will be producing the New PitsLigo Spoken Word Festival

He has two solo collections, Once Upon A Time There Was, Now There Isn't, & Solidarity (A short collection of rant political poems) , 2 Collaborative, Joined Up Writing 1 and 2, where over a 200 writers from around the globe are part of it (book 3 is almost done) and has well over 20 pieces published both online and in books from Australia, China, India USA, Canada and U.K. At the moment he is also getting ready to publish a book by 70 different writers aged over 70, and next year he will have another collection out, but this time his daughter will be part of it.

Saleha Chowdhury is an author of more than 80 Bengali novels, short stories, essays, poems, columns and two books of English poetry collection. Chowdhury was born in Rajshahi, Bangladesh in 1943. She was a lecturer in Dhaka University from `67 to 72. Then she moved to London with her family. She worked as a schoolteacher in London and now retired. Her favourite subject to depict is human being with their greatness and shortcomings. She has translated 25 English Books into Bengali. Peter Carry, Michael Ondatze, Roald Dahl, Pearl S Buck, Nelson Mandela, Hemingway, John Steinbeck, Marquez, Irving Stone among those. She received Annaya, Bangla Academy Probasi Lekhok Puruskar, Asraf Siddiqi Gold Medal, Lekhika Sanggha Puruskar, Ayesha Foyez Literary Award etc and for her English poems she got Merit award from Washinton DC and a Runners up prize.

Dr Bina Biswas, a former professor of English Language and Communications in TRR Group of JNTU(Hyderabad), holds a Ph D in English from Andhra University on Tagore's Prose Poems. She has authored thirteen books including 5 major translations and 2 poetry books. She has been a panelist in many national and international literary fests and conferences. She is a Tagore Scholar and a multilingual translator. She has been a jury member for Sahitya Akademi, New Delhi for two years. A facilitator with more than 25 years in teaching profession Dr Biswas has a consistent track record of success in training the students for Higher Education Verticals as Soft Skills Trainer in India and abroad. Currently, she manages a publishing house as the Founder CEO.

Mojaffor Hossain is a fiction writer of contemporary Bangla literature. Starting his career as a journalist and now working as a translator in the Bangla Academy, Dhaka, he has published six books packed with awe-inspiring short stories, which, in recent years, have attracted much acclaim from both general readers and literary critics. His signature style is using native realities as his settings and giving them magic-realistic or surrealistic colours. He has received Exim Bank-Anyadin Humayun Ahmed Award for his short story collection 'Atit Akta Bhindesh', Abul Hasan Sahitya Award for 'Paradheen Desher Swadheen Manushera' and Kali O Kalam Sahitya Award for Timiryatra, a novel. He has also been awarded Arani Sahitya Puraskar and Boishakhi Television Award for his stories. He is also known as a translator and literary critic and published 15 books so far. His other notable works are South Asian Diaspora literature, Pathe Bisleshane Bishwagalpo and Bishwasahityer Katha.

Leila Samarrai was born on October 19th 1976, in Kragujevac, Serbia. She writes poetry, short stories, and plays, her work largely containing the motives of fantasy and humour. Her debut collection of poetry 'The Darkness Will Understand' won the first prize of the competition organized by the student cultural centre of Kragujevac in 2002. She has had her work published in numerous local magazines, both in print and electronic form. Some of her notable works include the collection of short stories 'The Adventures of Boris K.' by Everest Media and (as co-author and critic) 'Poetry Against Terror: A Tribute to the Victims of Terrorism Kindle Edition'. Her works were published in Serbian, Hungarian and English. She has won numerous awards for her written works.

Louise Whyburd is a creative writer who lives in the South-west of England. Louise has always been creative, she studied a BTEC national diploma in Performing Arts during her college years and has also worked on a stained-glass window art project which is still displayed in the Steam Railway Museum in Swindon. She continued with her creativity into adulthood through her passion for cooking and art and rekindled her love of writing during lockdown. Louise has had poetry published in a selection of collective poetry books which have been sold across the world in several different languages. She has also written an article for a London published Hindu cultural magazine. Louise's writing is very much inspired by her life experiences and unique perspective on a vast array of subjects from nature to politics.

David Lee Morgan has travelled the world with his saxophone, as a performance poet and street musician. He has won many poetry slams, including the London, the UK, and the BBC Poetry Slam Championships. He has featured at St Anza, the international poetry festival in St. Andrews, Scotland, LINGO, Dublin's poetry and spoken word festival, and at the Isle of Wight festival. He is a longstanding member of the Writers Guild and holds a Ph.D. in Creative Writing from Newcastle University. He lives in London, grew up in the USA, was born in Berlin, and considers himself a citizen of the planet. He has been published in numerous magazines and anthologies and has two volumes of poetry published.

An author of ten books, **Gauranga Mohanta** has a PhD in English Literature. His books specially 'Robert Frost: A Critical Study in Major Images and Symbols' (2009) and 'A Green Dove in Silence: Forty Prose Poems in Translation' (2018) can spark a reader's interest. He worked for the civil service and lectured at several universities. Currently he teaches modern poetry in Bangladesh University of Business and Technology. He has been contributing articles, poems and translated works to magazines. He lives in Dhaka and endeavors to organize yearly Dhaka Translation Festival with the motto, 'Unite through Translation'.

Sarah James is a prize-winning poet, fiction writer, journalist, and photographer, also published as Sarah Leavesley. Her poetry has featured in the *Guardian*, *Financial Times* and Forward Prize anthologies, as well as in a café mural, on the BBC, on buses, city pavements and in the Blackpool Illuminations. Author of eight poetry titles, an Arts Council England funded multimedia hypertext poetry narrative > Room, two novellas and a touring poetry-play, her latest poetry collection is *Blood Sugar, Sex, Magic* (Verve Poetry Press, 2022), winner of the CP Aware Award Prize for Poetry 2021. She also runs V. Press, publishing award-winning poetry and flash fiction.

Bimal Guha (born 27 October 1952) is a Bangladeshi poet. He appeared on the Bangladesh literary scene in the 1970s. His themes revolve around the war of liberation and the eternal subjects of love, nature, motherland, mother-tongue, tradition, and modernity. Guha has 32 books to his credit; his works include poetry, research, travelogue, edited books and more than 100 articles on literature and culture. Uncompromising in life-struggles, Bimal never bends down to the ungraceful. Guha's first book of poems *Ahongkar, Tomar Shabdo* ("Pride, Your Words") was published in 1982. His style changed and he sought new perspectives from one volume to another. British poet Benjamin Zephaniah has remarked in an interview- "Bimal's poetry is so conversational, and he is also very passionate about the poetry of Bangladesh". He received a Bangla Academy Literary Award for poetry in 2022.

Brontë Elizabeth Page currently resides in London with her family and is completing her A Levels. As well as writing, she has aspirations of directing and her debut short film 'The Bathroom Mirror' will be premiering later this year.

Laura Whelton is a 45-year-old woman living in Cork city. She studied Fine Art and trained to be a chef in Fine Dining. She also studied Sociology, English and History of Art. She has some level 5 Fetac courses behind her also, she enjoys concerts, wine, music and literature. Laura has been published widely in Books, zines and blogs.

Obayed Akash was born on 13th of June 1973 at Sultanpur in Rajbari district of Bangladesh. He obtained his MA in Bengali language and literature from University of Dhaka. By now, he has been authored 41 books in his credit. Among them, 20 books are his original works of poetry. He has been editing an anti-stream Little Magazine called SHALUK (1999-) featuring literature, art and thoughts for twenty years. Professionally he is a journalist and presently works for prominent national newspaper The Daily Sangbad as its Literary Editor. So far has been honuored with *HSBC-Kali O Kalam Young Poet Award* in 2008. His remarkable poetry collections are *Poton Gunjone Vaase Kharosrota Chand (2001) Kuasha Uralo Jara* (2005), Patal Nirmaner Pronali (2006), Sorbonamer Sukhdukkho (2019), Prishthajure Sultanpur (2020) and Shreshtho Kabita (Selected Poems, 2019, Kolkata) and so on.

Pijush Kanti Barua is a quiet observer of life and nature and tries to listen to the tongues of time and the earth. He makes an effort to catch the melodies of nature in his poems. He was born on 10 October 1973, by the bank of *Karnafuli* in *Chattogram*, Bangladesh. His maiden book of poetry was *'Tomar Nibeetey Aunya Keu'* published in 2004. His '100 Poems', a collection of poems was published in December 2019. A card-poem collection was published in December 2010. A book offered to *Bangabandhu Sheikh Mujibur Rahman's* birth centenary was published in March 2020 named *'Janoker Aumrito Jeebon.'* He received the award of winner in Celebrating Life Lyrics Contest in 2009. He is a registered physician by profession.

Ashoke Kar was born on January 10th 1959, at Rajbari, in Bangladesh. Since adolescent, he has been engaged in writing and participated in cultural activities. During the

80's and 90's his poems, short stories, essays, and translation were published in Daily Newspapers, Magazines and Literary Anthologies. His writings became promising and dynamic. He created his own styles in writing and gained recognitions of his literary styles and contexts of the genre. Since 1999 he has been in the United States for his profession. During his tenure abroad, he managed his creative works in Bangla Literature and at the same time, become engaged in globalizing Bangla Literature via translations and participating global Literary organisations, in-home and abroad.

Thida Mommaitri is a college student from California. Writing is one of her passions and she channels her emotions through her writing process. She writes about heartbreak, her experiences growing up in an unstable home, the healing process in finding herself, and self-love journey. It is her outlet and hopes some of her prose/poetry can resonate with readers!

Tajalla Sattar belongs from Lahore, Pakistan and was born on 25th of November 1999. She started writing poetry as a hobby but gave up on it following her busy schedule. Now after a long pause she finally decided to give a proper attention to her poetic talent. Most of the time her poetry revolves around the light and shadowy aspects of human nature and the philosophy of life and death. She loves writing about the true essence of women that has long been forgotten and those dark parts of our society that most of us don't think about or simply ignore. She uses her poetry as a tool to express her feelings that normally she finds difficult to speak

Born on 3 April 1971 in Bangladesh, **Lipi Nasrin** obtained her master's degree from university of Rajshahi and Ph. D degree from the Institute of Biological Sciences under the same university. Currently she is serving as an Associate Professor of Botany at Satkhira Government College, Bangladesh. She wrote four poetry books in Bangla : 'Noisobder Nissongo Prohor(Lonely period of silence)' Godhuli Ronger Chhaya (The shadow of twilight)' 'Nilombon Madokota (Suspended obsession)'and 'Nistol Melancholy (Fathomless melancholy)' along with 'Rater brishti' (The Rain of Night), a collection of her short story. Her short stories and essays are being published in different literary magazines in Bangladesh and abroad. Some of her poems have been translated in German and published in an Anthology titled ' Ein Weg Zum Träumen-Teil-1(A way to dream part-1) from Austria. Her poems (translated) have also been published in UNBANGLA ANTHOLOGY, 'Under The Blue Roof' poems of Bengali poets from New York and POL (Poetry Out Loud) from London.

Dayal Datta is a Bangladeshi poet, born and raised there. In his poems, various inconsistencies of society, socialism, patriotism and international affairs are observed. Though he is a banker, he wrote numerous poems with a deep love for literature. In addition to writing in regular magazines, his writings in various international magazines and journals are popular.

Swakrito Noman is a writer of the Bangla language. He is one of the major writers in Bangladesh. He was born on 8 November 1980, in Bilonia of Porshuram Upazila under Feni district. Acquiring knowledge and writing are the goals he has set for himself. Among his published novels are Rajnoti, Begana, Hirokdana, Kalkeuter Sukh, Shesh Jahajer Adamera, Mayamukut, Ujanbashi and Mohuar Ghran. Pathak Samabesh has published his novels in two volumes and the short stories in one. He has books on other subjects too. He has been awarded with HSBC Kaali O Kalam award, Brac Bank- Samakal Humayun Ahmed Young Litterateur Award, Exim-Bank Humayun Ahmed Literary Award and with other honours. He is currently working at Bangla Academy which is the symbol of the intellectual excellence of the Bangali nation and of the cultural progression of the same.

Tareq Samin is a Bangladeshi secular-humanist author. He is the editor of the bilingual literary journal Sahitto. He has authored eight books. He edited two books of Anthology of International poetry which included 22 poets from 20 countries. His poems have been translated into more than 20 languages of which English, Spanish, Chinese, German, French, Italian are just a few to mention. His poems, short stories and articles have also been published in more than 25 countries. He received the 'International Best Poets Award-2020' from The International Poetry Translation and Research Centre (IPTRC), China and the Greek Academy of Arts and Writing. He has been awarded 'Honorable Mention' in Foreign Language Authors category for his poem

'Another Try' in 'The prize il Meleto di Guido Gozzano Agliè' poetry competition held on 12 September 2020 in Turin, Italy. In July 2021 he won Naji Naaman Literary Prize 2021. Tareq Samin is a Martin-Roth-Initiative Scholarship Alumnus. As a Martin-Roth-Initiative Scholarship holder, he was a guest writer in Goethe-Institute, Kolkata, India and Kathmandu, Nepal. In 2021, he was also an International guest writer in Château de Lavigny International writers-in-residence, Switzerland.

Kazi Rafi is a fiction writer in Bangladesh (B-1975). Kazi Rafi has eleven novels and six volumes of stories to his credit. He is a postgraduate in English literature. His first novel Blurred Dream of Sassandra compassionately depicted the simplicity of West African life. The gruesome description of the cannibal area and culture of the tribes enriches the reader's horizon of experiences. The art of story- telling, the similes, metaphor and Irony of life, characterization, subtlety of diction, thematic grandeur impressed the readers. For this novel the author was awarded with HSBC-Kali O Kolom Award-2010 which is one of the most prestigious award in Bangladesh and Bangla literature. He has fifteen more books published from Bangladesh and he received three more awards including 'Nirnay Gold Medal-2013' in his possession for the outstanding performance in the era of Novel and Short Stories.

Ashraf-ul Alam Shikder, (28 February 1964) was born in Bangladesh, is a full-time writer but even though designs pre-press, web, adverts; writes film scripts and poetry. He is the author of The Art of Writing a Script.

He has been working for a few advertising agencies since 1990 as Creative Director. He also worked for Ad-film, Tele-Drama, Music Videos, TV-programs and TV-films as a freelancer.

Farhod Eshanov was born in 1994 in Margilan, Fergana region of Uzbekistan. He is participant of the prose direction of the 2019-Zaamin seminar. His stories have been published in national newspapers and Russia.

Akhtar Hossain is a writer, play director, and columnist. His recent publication is a novel based on the true story of Bangladesh Liberation war hero Mr. Abu Sayeed Chowdhury. Akhtar Hossain has written and directed 13 plays. All of which were staged in Canada. In his childhood, Akhtar took part in Television and Radio programs. His first short story was published in the weekly Bichitra. He has a Bachelor of Social Science and a Master of Social Science degree from Dhaka University. Born in Dhaka, this freedom fighter of the Bangladesh liberation war has been living in Canada since 1987.

Aporanho Shushmito was born in Sylhet, Bangladesh. Starting writing in school life, he loved poetry and Rabindranath. For some time, writing was going on in the underground literary magazine. Run and jump in both prose and verse. He loves recitation, the beauty of the poem, the word-analogy, and the unbridled tension of the imagery may have set him in its colour of literature. Although studying Economics at the University of Chittagong, Bangladesh and programming in Canada did not separate him from the delightful love of poetry. He has acted in a short film. Poetry: *You Can, Aishwarya (2010), Alone Like President (2014)* Storybooks: *Zoo or Facebook and Other Stories (2016), Galpogulo (2019), Paromanu Galpo (2020)* Proverbs: *Mirror (2016).*

AKM Abdullah is a poet, story writer, editor (dashwebmag -Bengali and English) and the author of 8 books (6 poetry, 1 novel and 1 storybook; all are Bangla version). He was born in Bangladesh, currently living in the United Kingdom. More than a hundred English poems have been published in many anthologies and literary magazines. In A World of Despair (English Poetry Collection) to be published soon.

Eity Mithila is a young poet who was born on 6 February in Bangladesh. She obtained her master's degree in English literature from Begum Bodrunnesa Government Girls' College under Dhaka University. Composing poetry is her passion and genres in which she is more interested are spiritual and love poetry. Moreover, she achieved awards and certificates from different international literary platforms and her poems have been published in different anthologies of different countries.

Roksana Lais is a bohemian person who loves to travel and to know different cultures and people. Humanity and nature attract more than anything. Writing and painting is her passion. She loves to write fiction from the experience of life. She enjoys living a simple life with the love of nature and dislikes human cruelty, lies and dishonesty. Roksana Lais: Author, Poet, Story writer, and Novelist Born in Bangladesh now lives in Canada. Her published books: Looking for the Dream City, Bluewater in The Moonlight, At the Unknown Stream, In the middle, The Journey of light, Golden Light in Sraabon Moment, Lattar to Sky.

Sherzod Artikov was born in 1985 in the city of Marghilan of Uzbekistan. He graduated from Fergana Polytechnic Institute in 2005. He was one of the winners of the national literary contest 'My Pearl Region' in the direction of prose in 2019. In 2020, his first authorship book 'The Autumn's Symphony' was published in Uzbekistan by publishing house 'Yangi Asr Avlodi'. In 2021, his works were published in the anthology books called 'World Writers' in Bangladesh, 'Asia sings' and 'Mediterranean Waves' in Egypt, 'Emerging horizons' in India, 'Healing through verses 'in Canada in English language and his authorship book 'The autumn's symphony' was published in Spanish and English in Cuba by Argos Iberoamericana Publishing House.

Uday Shankar Durjay is a poet, essayist, and translator. He has been widely published in daily newspapers and magazines. Durjay was born in Bangladesh and currently lives in the UK. His first writing was published in 'Daily Jessore' in 1996. He studied Business Information Systems at the University of East London and MSc in Management at BPP University, UK. He is the author of *Likhe Rakhi Bishuddho Atmar Ratridin* (Keep writing the day night of the innocent souls, Bangla poetry collection), *Western*

Avenuer Aronnodin (The Woodendays of Western Avenue, Bangla translation of selected English poems), *Prabanddha Sangroho* (Collection of Bangla articles). Besides editing POL he is the editor of Spandan (A creative magazine of Bengali literature) as well. He has been awarded by Shahitto International Award for Literature in 2021.

Daniela Andonovska-Trajkovska (1979, Bitola, Republic of North Macedonia) is a poet, author, scientist, editor in chief of two prestigious literary magazines in North Macedonia, literary critic, doctor of pedagogy, university professor, a member of Macedonian Writers' Association, Macedonian Science Society – Bitola, Slavic Academy for Literature and Art in Varna – Bulgaria, Bitola Literary Circle, and she was president of the Macedonian Science Society Editorial Council (for two mandates). She has published two books of short stories, nine poetry books, literary critics, and over 100 scientific articles. Her four latest poetry books are: "House of Contrasts" (2019), "Electronic Blood" (2019), "Math Poetry" (2020) and "Walking on an Aerial Line" (2021). Her book "Electronic Blood" is translated into Arabic language and published in United Arab Emirates in 2021, and also was published in English in India in 2021. She has also co-authored one English poetry book "Dandelion Cadence" published in India. She has won several important awards for literature such as "Krste Chachanski (2018), "Karamanov" (2019), Macedonian Literary Avant-garde (2020), "Abduvali Qutbiddin" (2020, Uzbekistan), Premio Mondiale "Tulliola- Renato Filippelli" in Italy (2021), Award of excellence "City of Galateo - Antonio

De Ferrariis" (Italy) and "Aco Shopov" for poetry (the most important national poetry prize by Macedonian Writers' Association in 2021). Her works are translated and published into more than 40 world languages.

Mostafa Tofayel Hossain was born on 19 February 1954, at Kurigram, Bangladesh. Now he is settled at Rangpur, Bangladesh. He served in banking for about three decades. Currently, he has been teaching English literature in a university in Dhaka, Bangladesh. He is a poet, essayist, literary critic and translator. His contribution to Bengali literature rests on a travelogue of epics on Bangabandhu Sheikh Mujibur Rahman and the historic Independence Struggle of 1971. He is a cultural activist, both in Dhaka and Rangpur.

Chen Hsiu-chen is the executive editor of "Li" poetry magazine, has published books including "*Non-diary, 2009*", "*String Echo in Forest, 2010*", "*Mask, 2016*", "*Uncertain Landscape, 2017*", "*Promise, 2017*", "*Poetry Feeling in Tamsui, 2018*" , "*Fracture, 2018*", "*My Beloved Neruda, 2020*", "*Virus takes no rest, 2021*" and "*Encountering wth Cesar Vallejo, 2021*", some poems have been translated into more than 20 languages. She participated various national and international poetry festivals in Bangladesh, Macedonia, Peru, Tunisia, Chile, Vietnam, Romania and Mexico from 2015~2021, won "Morning Star Prize" from Peru in 2018 and "Naji Naaman Literary Prizes" from Lebanon in 2020.

Pran G Basak was born in 1955 at a remote village of Bengal. His parents moved to a small town from East

Bengal. Due to displacement his parents suffered a lot. In his childhood he worked in a weaving factory before going to school. Nevertheless, he worked as a part-time bidi worker during his student life. He finally moved to Delhi in 1980. Till now, he has published twenty collections of poems, one short-story volume and one satire in Bangla. He is one of the leading unputdownable younger writers of today's Delhi in Bangla poetry. He writes regularly in various little magazines published from different parts of India and Bangladesh. He received several literary awards.

Umapada Kar, a Bengali poet and essayist of contemporary Bengali New poetry. His magnificent and multidimensional poems objectify an object to refer its properties with a centrifugal journey by decentralizing consciousness. His poems create an imaginary space with the refracted light of his own experiences and aversive to any conventional poetry institute. He was born and brought up in Beharampur, Murshidabad in 1955 and presently lived at Kolkata, India. His first poetry book *Rituporber Nach* (Dance of Seasonality) published by Kobita Pakhshik in 1996 (Writing period-1979 – 1987). After that, he authored several poetry books: *Koyek Alokborsho Dure* (Few Light-years Away, pub: Roktomangso, 2002), *Porijayee Cholo* (Move on Migration, pub: Rourob, 2005), Bhanga Piyanor Paa (Leg of Broken Piano, Pub: Bhashabondhan, 2009), *Apor Bosonta* (The Other Spring, Pub: Kobita Campus, 2009), Dhonuk *Kothay Swar* (Vowels to Bow Words, Pub: 9ya Doshok, 2011) and so on. He is a hard-core traveller, loves theatre and songs, and loves Bengali's favourite adda. He believes that his poetry world gives him support in all his loses and traumas.

Shikdar Mohammed Kibriah is a global poetry promoter and literary figure. He is the president of Poetry and Literature World Vision. His published books are so far 17. His writings have been published into 35 languages in the world. He often takes part in world poetry conferences, festivals and anthologies and published in world class magazines, journals and newspapers. [Prodigy Published, USA]

Alok Biswas born in the state of West Bengal, India in 1959, Alok Biswas is a representative poet of the decade of Eighties. His first collection of poetry Blue Mirror was published in 1989. Till now he has published fifteen books of poetry and one collection of short stories. His different interpretations on contemporary Bengali poetry attract large number of intellectuals. He is the editor of a half-yearly literary magazine Kabita Campus since 1991 of which 92 issues have been published so far. He has also edited a good number of poetry anthologies of contemporary Bengali poetry. He works as English language and literature teacher at several private institutes.

Joanna Svensson – award winning Swedish poet, writer, and novelist. Has published 3 large fiction-novels, 8 books of poetry and participates in numerous anthologies all across the globe. The latest poetry book has been published in Arabic in 2021. A new American Poetry collection was published earlier this year where her poems taken a place. Joanna's fifteen short stories are going to be published soon. She is a member of Swedish Author's Society and The Polish Writers Abroad.

Saubhik De Sarkar (b.1976) is a Bengali poet and translator based in Alipurdar, West Bengal. His first book of poems 'Sheet O Bayosandhir Haspatal' was published in 1995. His poetry collections include 'Ekti Mridu Laal Rekha', 'Jatrabari', 'Dakhalsutra', 'Anugato Buffer'. He has translated Saadat Hasan Manto, Federico Garcia Lorca, Julio Cortázar , Roberto Bolaño, Namdeo Dhasal, Martin Espada and Rudramurthy Cheran into Bengali. He is the recipient of 'Kabita Pakshik Award', 'Mallar Award', 'Mallika Sengupta Award', 'Shaluk Award' and participated in Sangam House International Writers Residency Programme (2019).

Hussein Habasch is a poet from Afrin, Kurdistan. He currently lives in Bonn, Germany. His poems have been translated into English, German, Spanish and so on. His books include: Drowning in Roses, Fugitives across Evros River, Higher than Desire and more Delicious than the Gazelle's Flank, Delusions to Salim Barakat, A Flying Angel, No pasarán (in Spanish), Copaci Cu Chef (in Romanian), Dos Árboles and Tiempos de Guerra (in Spanish), Fever of Quince (in Kurdish), Peace for Afrin, peace for Kurdistan (in English and Spanish), The Red Snow (in Chinese), Dead arguing in the corridors (in Arabic) Drunken trees (in Kurdish), Boredom of a tired statue (in Kurdish), Flor del Espinillo (in Spanish) and A Rose for the Heart of Life, Selected Poems (in English).

Recipient of the Great Kurdish Poet Hamid Bedirkhan Award, awarded by the General Union of Kurdish Writers and Journalists. As well as the international "Bosnian Stećak" award for poetry, awarded by the Bosnia and Herzegovina Writers Union.

Masudar Rahman is a Bangladeshi poet. He was born on 01 September 1970, Joypurhat, Bangladesh. Rahman has been writing last 30 years. He has published 13 books in a different category; ten of them are poetry collections.

Sumana Ray has been a prolific writer since her college days. Born and raised in Tripura, she now works and lives in Mumbai. Her poems and stories get regularly published in magazines and journals. She has also written four books titled Uran, Jolorob, Rangiye Diye Jao, and Imon Rater Kuasha. All of these have been very well received by the readers. She has been invited and honoured at International literary festivals, wherein she has presented her works to an audience of distinguished personalities from the world of Bangla literature. She studied Mathematics and loves to play outdoor and indoor games. She is fond of music, travelling and she enjoys long rides on her bicycle. Sumana's determination is admired by many as she works very hard to maintain the work-life balance. She has come a long way but remains passionate about writing and continues to pursue excellence.

S. M. Quamrul Bahar (Writer's Name: Quamrul Bahar Arif) is a poet and literary editor of Bangladesh. He has published thirteen books with inspiring poems which have attracted general readers. He is also an editor of little magazine named 'MRIDONGGO'. He is also a good literary and cultural organizer.

Antje Stehn, Germany poet, visual artist, art curator, German PEN Zentrum. Co-editor of poetry Magazines TamTamBumBum, Los Ablucionistas and Archer, member of the directive committee of Piccolo Museo della Poesia, Italy. She is curating the art-poetry project 'Rucksack a Global Poetry Patchwork' which involves more than 250 international poets.

Prottoy Hamid is a poet, story writer and translator. He was born on 27 February 1980 in Naogaon, Bangladesh. He completed his Honours and master's degrees in English from University of Rajshahi. He is now serving as the head of the dept. of English, Bangladesh Army University of Engineering & Technology (BAUET), Natore, Bangladesh. He has published 12 books covering poetry, short stories, rhymes and translation. He received various awards from home and abroad as recognition of his writings. He is the editor of a little mag titled *Hyphen*.

Mariia Starosta lives in Ukraine in the city of Lviv. Author of two poetry books "Two Worlds" and "A Woman With The Smell of Smoke". Plans to publish the third bilingual collection "Reflections of A Woman". She teaches Ukrainian language and literature at the Lviv Linguistic Gymnasium. Married, raising a son and a daughter.

Mili Roy born on 19 October in Moulvibazar, Sylhet. Roy had her upbringing and schooling in Feni district town. The poet completed SSC and HSC from Feni Government Girls High School and Feni Government College respectively. She earned honors and master's degree from Comilla Victoria Government University College. She loves recitation, music and needlework in addition to her enduring passion for poetry. She has also been an avid reader since her childhood. She began writing short fictions while studying in school. They were, however, confined to the pages of her diaries due to her qualities of being a little shy. After a long hiatus, she returned to the world of poetry. Her poems have been continuously published in various newspapers, online journals, quality little magazines and anthologies at home and abroad for the last two years.

Anindita Mitra was born on 17 May 1982 and is influenced by the philosophy of Rabindranath Tagore. She believes in humanism and detests fundamentalism. Mitra writes poetry, stories and articles. *Ebong Aparajita* (Bangla) is a collection of short stories, published in 2018. She lives in Kolkata, India now.

Mahfuza Anonya is a poet of the indistinctive arena. She was born on 20 September 1982 in Bangladesh. Poetry is the inspiration for daily life. Her premier Bangla poetry collection 'Sonali Ashuk' (2019) has been written in postmodern genera. Poetry readers and critics appreciated her literary aspects. In a short interval, she published her second poetry collection "Kamarto Nagorer Kamiz" (2019). Her poetry draws the attention of poetry lovers and critics for its extraordinary depth and intellectual approaches. Her third Bangla poetry collection named "Abong Navir Kenya" is an intellectual expression of the deep sense of joy and sorrow of individuals as well as the approaches to the whole human insights. Her next Bangla poetry endeavours are "Ashi Torrrar Choumbon" (2021) and "Trevuz Ful Sonibar Fote"(2022).

Aliza Khatun was born on February 2nd 1981, in the village of Arunbari in the Chapainawabganj district of Bangladesh. She studied M.Sc in Mathematics at Jagannath University, Dhaka, Bangladesh. Aliza Khatun is the eldest of four siblings. She is the mother of one son. Living in Satkhira district headquarters, she works at a humanitarian international organisation & quot; Rishilpi handicrafts limited & quot; as an executive HR. She published poetry: Noishabdo Chhona Jal, Modhyarater Khame, Bhangonkal, Srabon Janala, Rodmakha Chitthi, Gahine Daho, Aradhya Pother Dike, Mumurshu Mokame; and published proses: Borgamati, Vatir Tane, Agun Gonja Mati, Roktosamudra O Ekush Akkhyan.

Sutanuka Mondal born in a Bengali family in West Bengal, she is an English Teacher, a freelance Content and Ghost writer and a budding Bilingual poet. She attended Carmel Convent School and completed M.A. in English and Culture Studies followed by a professional course in Teaching Methodology. An avid reader, a passionate writer she also enjoys listening to music and preparing new dishes. Through her poetry she manifests the picture of real social disorder to the reader. Has work has been featured in Afrobizgermany, Lipi Magazine, Story Mirror and published in other national and international journals and anthologies.

Mridha Alauddin was born in February 1978. Kangshi, Wazirpur, Barisal. His writings are regularly published in the country's national daily newspaper and littlemag. Mridha is a rhythm-conscious poet. The first poem of Mridha 'The Mind Goes to The Sun'-(poems). Published by Rel Gachh, Moghbazar, Dhaka-1217, (Poetry-Revelation: 2005). 2. 'Next Winter men Will become Sunlight'-(poems). Publisher: Barnes and Noble, 122 5th Avenue # 2 Nwe York, NY-10011. (Poetry-Revelation: 2020). 3. 'Next Winter men Will become Sunlight'-(poems). Published by Mohammad Liaquatullh of Student Ways, 9 Banglabazar, Dhaka-1000. (Poetry-Revelation: 2021). 4. 'Butterflies have become some fishes' (poems). Published by Mohammad Liaquatullh of Student Ways, 9 Banglabazar, Dhaka-1000. (Poetry-Revelation: 2020). A few poisons needed (Doha's poems). Published by Mohammad Liaquatullh of Student Ways, 9 Banglabazar, Dhaka-1000. (Poetry-Revelation: 2021). Awards and Honors: Atish Dipankar Gold Medal. Bangabhumi Literary Honor, Bangabhumi Sahitya Parishad. Pinnacle Literary Medal, Pinnacle Littlemag. Crest of the Bengali Muslim Literature Association and gold medal. Edit: A poem (Littlemag is out of about 5 numbers, meaning littlemag is closed). The editorial of Mridha has been published by late poet Misbahul Islam Chowdhury of Sylhet, 'Sher Shah' (an epic) by Mishahul Islam Chowdhury. Mridha is currently working in the Bhorer Kagoj newspaper.

Hrishikesh Goswami (India Book of Records Holder for Poetry and Creative Endeavour of the Month April 2021 by The Assam Tribune) is a contemporary naturalistic poet from Assam, India who specialises in writing about nature and realism coalescing fiction and non -fiction in a sophisticated blend. Hrishikesh's poems have been critically analysed by Fruit Journal Manchester (UK), Acorn (a journal of contemporary haiku), The Leading Edge Magazine, *BreakBread Magazine* and has been published by The Assam Tribune's Horizon and Planet Young, NEZINE (an online magazine), Noverse Foundation and FoxGales Publishers, Poem hunter-The World's Poetry Archive, Guwahati Grand Poetry Festival, Cultural Reverence and many more.

Nivedita Lakhera born and raised in New Delhi, India. She grew up in a very loving and supportive family. Currently she lives in California. Nivedita Lakhera, M.D., is a board certified-internal medicine doctor. She has more than a decade of experience in Inpatient Medicine. She is considered to be one of the leading feminist contemporary poets and a staunch advocate of gender equality in all spheres of life, especially medicine and technology. She is a prolific writer, having written 4000 poems and prose, besides having created a massive body of artwork - all while being dedicated to her professional practice of medicine. Lakhera has published two poetry and art books- Pillow of Dreams, and, I Am Not A Princess, I Am A Complete Fairytale.

Part Two

Short Stories

D. A. "Roarshock" Wilson

Labyrinth

A.. A… imagined he was in the Labyrinth at the top of Nob Hill next to California Street sometime during the existence of San Francisco. He wasn't sure if this meditative walk was really present, a past memory, or a future precognition. He was not sure if he was the author of a yarn sitting at a high-rise desk somewhere else along California Street researching and writing. Perhaps that was a fancy of his meditating mind that he was a character in the Story of the Labyrinth as interpreted by his own meta-self, but he also thought maybe he was some totally other guy far away in time and place with no knowledge of Labyrinth or meditation, or overarching creators of creation. Someone who called bullshit on all mystical notions and multiple levels of dimensions of reality. All that was not clearly and literally "true" rejected out of hand when only solids were perceived and the smoke and mirrors behind the veils of form were not noticed at all. The mystery of existence understood not as a journey through Labyrinth, but as a specific game of cards the outcome of which being determined by the luck of the draw and the skill with which the hand was played. Alternative outcomes can only be considered in so far as they remain within the realm of mathematical probability. Whoever this literal fellow

might be or might have been, he was certainly not A..
A… of California Street fame imagining himself in
Labyrinth. What visions whirling, what stories unfolding
in cosmic drama within and without. He had expected
solitude and calmness of mind rather than a churning
chaos of realities and fantasies. It felt like a maze, but
A.. A… knew that the single path of Labyrinth was
different than multiple branches and sometimes dead
ends encountered in a maze, but how could a single path
exist in multiverse? Labyrinth was first built at Knossos
by Daedalus for King Minos of Crete as a cage to
imprison the Minotaur. So cunning was the design the
Daedalus himself could barley escape it. That first
Labyrinth was a maze, not a singular path, but it
occurred to A.. A… that every maze that could be trans-
versed, passed through and escaped, was actually a
singular path however complicated it may seem. Stephen
Daedalus, a fictional version of the Author of Ulysses
(who also previously appeared in A Portrait of the Artist
as a Young Man), makes his Labyrinth journey through
the maze of Dublin on a fictional June 16, 1904 arriving
at the center in the home of Leopold and Molly Bloom
before disappearing out into the night. Here comes
everybody in James Joyce's last book Finnegans Wake
and the Labyrinth contained within the maze expands
across dreams and all the times and dimensions of dream
space. A.. A… long admired the brilliance of the
drunken Irishman and ingenious punster. "The pun is the
highest form of humor." Joyce reportedly had said. A..
A… always admired Joyce's fierce dedication to his
work and absolute certainty of his own greatness. He,
with great dignity, lived off patronage and lived large

because he knew he was a Great Man doing world changing work. A.. A… had known since childhood that he was a poet. As he grew up he learned he was either not a driven enough, or great enough, poet to attract rich patrons who would support him (his father had once took him aside and pointedly told him that he did not have a patron and had better find a regular job), so he spent much more time working unrelated jobs to pay his rent, feed and educate his children. However, the more he studied the Jazz Age scene, the more he learned of the skepticism with which some of Joyce's contemporaries had viewed his dignified begging to support his extravagant lifestyle. A.. A… also realized in his own life as time went on the insights, knowledge and deepening of his poetic understanding gained in every job and situation of his checkered career in the mundane world. This trip through Labyrinth was not calming and focusing his mind on a singular path of a particular color. Unlike a seated meditation concentrating on a mantra or the flow of breath, this slow walk was sending his imagination soaring with James Joyce and the Lost Generation, with a descendant of Stephen Daedalus (Joyce's creation) through the sprawling malls of Dublin, California over there beyond the East Bay hills, south of the mighty peaks of Mount Diablo. Daedalus was the father of Icarus and fashioned wings for them both from feathers and wax, but Icarus flew too high — the heat of the sun melting the wax — and he fell into the sea and drowned. The Labyrinths of California Street were laid out at Grace Cathedral (direct descendant of San Francisco's Grace Church, founded 1849) replicating the medieval labyrinth of Cathédrale Notre-

Dame de Chartres in France. Among its enthusiasts was Phil Lesh — noted sacred geography student — who featured it on an album of his workcalled There and Back Again (2002), and that thought landed at the furry feet of Bilbo Baggins and the road of Middle Earth that goes on forever, curling clear, or lost in grey haze like rings of Professor Tolkien's pipe weed smoke. Back from reverie, A.. A... was walking along California Street having just topped the hill, passing Grace Cathedral at about half past four on a cold December morning. Shuffling along towards him and passing by was the Old Man of the Mountain. For at least a quarter century A.. A... had seen him go there and back again up and down California Street (only the Smiley Guy of Polk Street was a longer tenured homeless presence in the neighbourhood). With a rush of revelation, A.. A... realized that the Old Man of the Mountain was walking a personal Labyrinth, just like he always did, up and down the steep slopes of California Street. Labyrinth, maze, sacred geography, all existing everywhere in all times and spaces, accessible to any and all. ~ D. A. "Roarshock" Wilson

James Tian

The Yorkshire Christmas Cat On Thanksgiving

If someone can knocked on and get answered a
stranger's door, even hadn't received the real comfort or
a smiling face, he or she will be still the luckiest one in
this world. At this critical time of autumn and winter, in
addition to the loneliness, only the aeolian bells were
fiddled from time to time, the women who entered their
home always opened the attic windows to have a look to
those laundry line brackets. It's the normal life that we
hope forever, as ordinary as it should be, and floated on
the street with occasional emotions.

Today's the fourth Thursday of November, an unusual
day in this country. Yoki is preparing a turkey and the
most cutest pumpkin pies in home now. A simple shabby
hut but a truly natural place. She prepared it not only the
dinner, but also wanted to build a kind of warmth. Even
if her husband Lyle didn't ready to get this surprise, she
must jump in with both feet to use the warmth that from
her brain to conceal the shyness of this residence and
much blanks in no gifts given.

Lyle's a postman in this town. He went out early and
came back at dusk, always hoped to make up for some of
the shortcomings of this family around this warm
candlelight. The injured nerve is now so brittle that he
can perceive the sound of snow falling on the palm of

his hand, so for this special day, he had been looking forward to its coming as soon as possible. For the time, only less than a few hours away from today, he became nervous. There had nothing to give his wife as the expression, and only the falling body can be sent to home indeed. Cause of this, with two empty fists, he went to the farthest block to send the last letter. There'll be fewer soul writing letters in the future, and the life which full of the poetic beauties will fly away too. Oh poor fish,where's his future destination? He just thought it in deep, in dragging a heavy shadow.

It was about five o'clock when Lyle got home, he knocked on his door, and Yoki went to ask for it then, later his slightly thin leather bag was lied on sofa's back in silence. She just smiled to him, "Today's weather is in mood darling." Surprised from her usual loser's face, but more excited enough to let him go on it, "Oh ya, it's awful. The wind had made us lose feeling in fact, just like burning a handful of firewood without any feelings of much haha." She kept the warmth, "Of course." And they were busying for themselves in doing this. She took care of the food on the table and sorted it out again. After all, it was important to pay attention in more-so much foods can kill the hunger for a week of them, it seemed shabby enough, but a solid truth too. And then, the prayers are also very important tonight for them. He went to their room to change the wearing. While he changed the clothes, she had lit two candles which were unevenly tall. There was a thick layer of oil on the candlestick, and the two waxes shed tears and looked at the people who'll perform in the final song of Thanksgiving, burned the time in the hourglass. She also arranged the covers and sat on the seat by the door,and the seat clicked like a sigh.

All in ready now, but one of this blessed couple still in his side. The Bible was also waiting on the table, holding its breath too. The sound of "click"by the door was closed, followed by a sound of his footsteps.

"I'm sorry, a bit slow this time." He wiped his hands, with the cold wind from outside. Just as usual, she took his seat by the door, to let him avoid the noise of the rumour of course, he knew her temper in well, and didn't want to force her anyway.

"Doesn't matter. "She smiled and let her husband sit down, even though the candles' light weren't enough to make them catch each other's looking clearly.

And now the dinner was carrying on. Before the beginning, the prelude was very important as they knew-that was the prayers. Both closed their eyes and supported the "Bible" with their hands. About five minutes later, they stared at each other at first and then began to enjoy this like luxurious night. Apart from eating and staring at this moment, without anything else, even if some conversations. The door was screamed and aggrieved by those wind always visited them from time to time and coughed to express the peace of this night. Tonight, in this room, there's a book of "Bible" that's dilapidated enough, every night after its oppressed by their hands, always be accompanied by the wind and lightness. And now, there're two tearful candles interacting but without any eye contact. Perhaps something is missing in this hut now the moment, but something what is more too here again.

It was in the midnight when Yoki got ready and entered the bedroom, and Lyle had gone to the wonderful dream already in this time, she knew that he was busy the whole day today very well, although she did too, she covered him with the quilt and sighed again quietly. Looked back through the window at the transparent sky with a few ribbon-tip marks, it was looking at the world coldly now. She went to the bed and wanted to turn off the switch of the lamp placed on the old desk, suddenly she found that a note was pressed under the base. She took the slightly pitiful note and opened it, only some words looking at her tenderly, but more tears to be surged in seriously: Good night my baby!

Fin Hall

Small Ad

It started with a small ad in the local paper. I must point that you should read the word 'paper' quite reservedly. It is not unknown for this erstwhile rag to recirculate stories, repeating an article a fortnight or so after its initial appearance. In fact, if truth be told, and I will endeavour to do so, that on one recent occasion it was noted that the same story was not just printed in a column on the front page, but also verbatim on one of the inner pages. Albeit in a different layout. But the same story nonetheless.

I digress. Having read the sports' pages first, as is my wont, I was working my way through the paper, Chinese Style I believe, towards the front of the paper: when my eye was caught by the small ads. Well, actually one ad in particular. Nestled as it was between, 'For sale; 1 aquarium, 3ft by 5ft. c/w pump, filter, and two weeks' supply of fish food. May sell separately. Phone 01555 623326. After 6 pm, but before 1030 pm.' (I still ponder what happened to the fish). And, ' IKEA 3 shelf unit. For sale. Unused. Incomplete. PO box621'

I have no idea why, on this particular day I would happen to be stopped in my tracks by a small ad, least alone this one, but something about it intrigued me. It read, ' For sale, gents' leather, bomber style jacket.

Brown. Medium fit. V.G.C. Call 01555 414114. Quick sale preferred. ' Nothing unusual either in the wording, nor the phone number. In fact, the whole thing reeked of, ordinary. Very much so. Maybe even sad could be used. But as circumstances would have it, my eyes kept returning to the section. Even after I had turned the page and moved into reading something different. A much more interesting article about a woman who found a snake in her child's pushchair. I could not but help myself returning to this ad, and 01555 414114, in particular. I mean, it's not as if I needed a bomber jacket, even a leather one. .

Following on with my curiosity, I dialed the number. It rang for just a short time, and the voice that answered captured my attention, making me all the more interested if following through with this. Not soft, not harsh, it wasn't what you'd call sensual either but..."
Hello,414114"
"Ah, yes," slightly caught off guard," I'm calling about the paper, tonight's paper."
"The add? In a paper" came the soft spoken, puzzled sounding voice.
"Yes, the paper. The ad for the leather jacket?
Still puzzled sounding, I could hear the person at the other end of the line murmuring to themselves. I was just about to hang up thinking that I had better things to do with my day, when the tone at the other end underlying picked up.
"Ah yes, the ad. The leather jacket was it?"
" Indeed." I replied " The bomber jacket."

" The bomber style jacket." Came the immediate response.

" Yes, that's the one. Can I ask, is it still available?"

" Available? Yes, it is still here. Are you interested in it?"

Mmm. The question. Confused me. Why would I be calling them up for it if I wasn't interested? I didn't let it distract me though, it only added to the mystery. " Yes, yes, of course, I am. Is it at all possible to come and see it today?"

" Today, today, depends, do you live local?"

Another odd question. Local? Local to where,? Instead, I told her where I stayed, and she informed me that her address is only a relatively short distance away.

"Great, can I come and see it today? It is only a short walk away from me. Oh, by the way, there is no price in the ad, how much are you asking for it?"

"Good question, mm, I haven't really thought about the price, but I promise you that you won't be in a hurry to ask for your money back. That I can assure you. I won't bleed you dry for sure.''

Another perplexing reply. But I shrugged it off and informed the seller that I will make my way over.

Hanging up the phone, I made my way to the front door of my flat, taking my red blazer off the pegs by the apartment exit. Although the weather was fine, not sunny but not cold, it had been raining quite heavily very recently and there were remnants of puddles here and there.

Walking along the relatively quiet streets, deep in thought. Puzzling over what I am doing and who is the mysterious seller. Being lost in thought, I wasn't aware of the car heading toward me at some speed, and coincidentally when I approached the next junction, the vehicle was intending to turn into the corner. Luckily the noisy engine and the sound of the driver applying his brakes to make the manoeuvre. I automatically reacted by stepping further back onto the pavement. The car however either didn't notice or deliberately drive into the puddle at the side of the kerb, splashing some water on me. Not a lot, thankfully, but enough to leave a couple of dark patches on my jacket.

It wasn't long till I reached my destination, which was a normal-looking bungalow, but situated behind a tall and overgrown hedge, shading any light that could enter the garden. The garden which is fairly untidy and accentuated by about a dozen or so sections of the plot where the ground was not flat but raised a little and in various states of regrowth.

The front door, although not quite in standing with the area, was not different enough to stand out. The doorbell made no obvious noise when I pushed it, but just when I was about to push it again, the door opened and the same almost sultry voice that I heard on the phone said, " Oh, hi there. I presume you have come for the leather, bomber style jacket. Please come in."

I stepped over the portal and into the vestibule. The door closed behind me.

It started with a small ad, tucked away between two equally inconsequential other ads. The ad read. For Sale, Gents, Medium, Red Blazer type jacket, V.G.C. Except small muddy, damp stain on the front. Call 01555 414114. Quick sale preferred.

Saleha Chowdhury

Mira Sayal's Rose Garden

Mira Sayal was working in the garden. She was plucking the weeds and storing in a bin bag. Tomorrow is Thursday, the binman from the council is supposed to come to empty the bins. The blue bin is for the recyclable glass, paper and plastic, while the green bin was for food, garden leaves, weeds or grass. The black bin was there for the other garbage items. She was having a backache while plucking weeds by stooping low over the ground. She stood up straight for a while and stretched her back. She raised her hands and stood on her toes for a bit. Then, she looked at the roses. Many rose plants were there. Some of them were old, while some were newly planted. She had bought the tubs from the nursery and placed them here. The sky was clear. It would not rain today. But, can you really trust London's weather?

"Barkha, could you take me to Daisy-Dahlia Nursery please" Her daughter listened to her. She lived in a small flat on her own and works in an office. Still, she took her mother to Daisy-Dahlia Nursery one day. On that day, Mira Sayal had bought two sacks of fertilised soil, a big miracle gro and two new rose plants. On their way back, both of them had icecreams. They chatted like two old friends for a while. That miracle of fertilized soil and miracle gro were now shining brightly in her garden. Mira felt great whenever sat on a chair and looked around at the flowers. The leaves were playing by themselves. A wonderful sight indeed! Her son Abinash had asked, "What would you like to have for your birthday ma?"

Pensioner Mira Sayal replied like a child, "A few chairs and a big umbrella over there for me baba!" To make her happy, son brought two chairs, a table, and a big umbrella with red flower prints. The happiness of getting these gifts brought tears to Mira's eyes. Now, she sat on the chair alone as her husband could not move much after having a major stroke. He had roamed around in the garden once or twice, but he could not sit here for long for backache. Mira sat in the garden with a two-band radio. She had either a sewing frame or a book with her. She liked the melody of tunes played by the classic FM radio. Even though she did not know about musical notations, but she did not have any trouble enjoying music. It is very soothing. Her daughter bought her three solar lights worth 10 pounds. At night, the light glowed softly. Mira listened to the music in that soft glow and felt that there is no one as happy as her in the entire London city. Classic FM was playing something that made her tearful. Sometimes. it made her happy and her heart flutters like a butterfly. Mira was alone in the rose garden. She had never thought of being happy with someone else in the garden. Although the moon was up, could it even illuminate London? Moonlight had been in exile long ago. But she did not even long for that moonlight when the solar light was on. The solar light seemed to enlighten the area. Her neighbour's garden had a solar lamp as well. Mira looked at that garden. Nope! it did not have much care. Only some apple and cherry trees. No one thought about flowers in that garden. An old lady lived there alone. Tormented with backache, knee pain, she did not have time for gardening. This eighty-year-old neighbour named Rosemary had been living alone for many years. A nurse came to see her twice a week, shopped for her, fed her medicines and helped her to have shower. There were many Rosemaries in Britain, who lived all alone. Maybe one day, she would either go to the old people's home or floating dead in the bathtub. Then someone would discover her dead body. After that someone new would buy the house and make a big garden. Mira looked at the red rose plant and said-"Barkha, see how many flowers the plant has now". Her rose plants had names, Barkha, Shanta, Hariyali, Abinash, Tinni, Anandi and many other names like these. And the plant that bloomed only yellow roses, Mira named it Asad. Who's name was that? Mira Sayal smiled to herself. There was a young man named Asad in their neighbouring house. The name Asad was given after him. Mira had not seen that face for the last fifty years or more. But still she remembered him. The lovely young man who used to play a mouth organ and juggled oranges or rubber balls with his hands. If he did not find anything, he used to juggle with tomatoes and potatoes. She still remembered him. Is there any special reason for it? Mira Sayal smiled on her own. A sixty seven year old face lighted up with a smile..

She had put a black wig on her own hair. Most of her hair had fallen out. She did not feel good to see herself in the mirror. That's why, a few years back, she went to the shop stealthily to buy a bob cut wig. Now, no one remembered her real look with less hair. Barkha had bought another wig from Malta. That can be used with a bun. She used that bun wig whenever she wore a saree to attend a party. Some people wondered why her hair was short one day, and with bun other day. Eventually, they knew the truth and no one asked any more question about it. And one day Mira sharply told a nosey woman - "Stop asking questions about my hair." There were many Mira Sayals like her, who wore wigs or hairpiece at an old age.

Haridas Sayal was at the door-"Mira, your phone".

Barkha maybe! Thought Mira. She wiped her hands and entered the room

"Who's speaking please?"

"I'm Shudha."

"Shudha?"

" Yes. A few days back, we've met on the bus, isn't it? I am that Shudha. Shudha Patel."

Mira Sayal remembered her. "So, what's up Sudha?"

"You'd told me that you were looking for a green rose plant for your garden. Found that! Yesterday, I went to the nursery and found green roses. I've brought one for you, the rose-plant is in the tub. Me and my daughter Padma found the plant. She bought one for her garden and I bought one for you."

"Green? I have red, white, pink, yellow, but not the green rose."

Shudha replied, "Reddish-green. Not the stark green. Mira, I think you know that different colours of roses have different meanings, right?"

"What type of meaning?" Mira pretended not to know the meanings and let her talk.

"Red means passion or love. White is for purity or sacredness. Pink is for love and tenderness. And the yellow one is the symbol of love that has ended. Or you can say, a symbol of being separated."

"What about the reddish-green rose?"

"It means Celebration of life." Shudha gave her a hearty laugh.

Both of them had worked in a shop for a while. Shudha Patel from Gujarat. Shudha was a very ordinary person, not a daughter of a senior police officer as Mira Sayal. Maybe her father used to be a farmer and she was married to an ordinary man as well. Her husband was not a technician as Mira's. He perhaps worked in a leather coat factory. Mira was not sure if he still worked there. Mira was now a retired clerical office of the civil service. She had met Shudha while doing an odd job in a shop.

Shudha was now 67 years old. She looked the same as before. Only her pain of arthritis increased. The feet looked swollen. She was wearing a saree with big green flowery pattern, like most of the other girls of Gujarat. Probably, they were from the same area. Some of these girls had tattoos on their hands and legs. Shudha had a tattoo on her palm. When she met her on the bus, she sat beside her and chatted. There was no showing off in Mira's behaviour or speech. A very simple Mira Sayal. She herself had forgotten that she had completed her M.A. in Urdu Literature. Even though the degree was of no use in Britain, there was always a literature and music lover inside her. She liked to listen to classic FM, buy records, roam around book shops and often returned home after selecting books from the library. Her choices did not match with Shudha's. Still, when they met on the bus or street, they talked about pension, blood pressure, diabetes or their kids. The thought of Shudha bringing a rare rose plant made Mira very happy. Reddish-green rose which is also the celebration of life! The symbol of life. Shudha told her about the plant in such a way that Mira began to think about a name already.

"Who was on the phone?" Haridas asked while watching T.V.

"You don't know her." Mira went back to the garden again. She didn't approve of this nature of Haridas. He wanted to know about the 14th generations of any person on the phone. Well, she never worried about Haridas' phone calls. Maybe, staying imprisoned at home had made him like this. "But anyway, there is no use in thinking all these."

While weeding, she brought a mug of tea and sat under the umbrella. The scorching summer light was covered with a shadow of clouds. The sun had hidden itself. She was enjoying the time, it seemed that the soft cloud with sudden rain will come anytime. Barkha was full of white flowers. Abinash was shining bright with red roses. Bindia had pink flowers and Asad bloomed a very big yellow rose. Lovely Asad who juggled with oranges. They had lived as neighbours for four years in Dehradun. Thirteen, fourteen, fifteen, and just when she was sixteen, they were transferred to Bombay. Her father was a senior police officer. After that, she had never met Asad. Now, she named a rose plant after Asad. Why? Who could tell why. Yellow is the symbol of "Goodbye Forever", the last meeting or the end of a relationship.

Barkha kept on telling these things to her. Maybe Barkha was in love with a white guy. She never shared all these in detail with her mother Mira. In the same way, Mira was unaware of the trouble that Abinash was having with his partner, a Welsh girl. A black bird perched on the wall. Sometimes birds like this would come to the garden. Two apple trees were standing there side by side, first they filled with blossoms, and then blossoms became small apples. Mira did not think much about the apple tree. She used to think more about the roses.

It seemed that she had started to read Mirza Ghalib's poetry after a long time. All these years, she was busy with her office and did not have time to read all of this. But now retired, Ghalib, Hafiz, Jalal Uddin Rumi, Fayaz Ahmed had returned to her life. She did not write any literary work, but she had a passion for literature and also roses. Along with that she admired some western literature too.

She put all the rubbish gathered in a corner into the big bin. Then she would throw them into the bin outside. Mira Sayal had turned 67 on 5th March this year. That's the time when she got the umbrella, table, two chairs and three solar lights as gifts. Horidas had crossed 74 and stepped into 75. He could not move around much because of a cardiac arrest five years back. He did not talk much either. But he sometimes went extreme with his investigations on what Mira was doing, with whom she was talking to.

Mira Sayal panned rotis for Haridas and some vegetables from last night with some curd. She had some tomato soup and a slice of bread She had taken off the homely clothes and put on a good Salwar Kameez. Also, she did not forget to take an umbrella with her. One could not really rely on the weather of the London. It was sunny now, and then suddenly it started to rain. Sometimes it was freezing cold. And then hot and sunny. In London, no one could keep up with the weather. She had a book in her bag to return it to the library. She liked the book by Anita Desai. Still now, Desai did not get the Booker Prize. But she deserved it, thought Mira. Today she did not issue any new book.

Shudha lived at Griffin road. It was 15 minutes by bus or on foot 30 minutes. Mira Sayal loved walking. She chose a short-cut to Shudha's, In due time she reached No 36. Griffin Road. It was Shudha's own house. None of Shudha's sons or daughters lived with her. Mira had never come to this house before. Today, she arrived to collect the green rose plant. Mira rang the doorbell Ding Dong! The door was opened by someone else. That means Shudha had a tenant in her house. Mira would never do that. She would never rent her rooms to a stranger. Never. She did not like anyone else to interfere with the freedom she had inside the house. Her daughter Barkha came once or twice a week to stay with her. Abinash's did not stay with her. One of the rooms had books and it was her favourite room. When Abinash came, he preferred to stay in the room next to the living room, downstairs. There was no bathroom upstairs, and for that, he stayed downstairs.

Shudha came forward to welcome Mira with a big smile. She took her to the small living room. Mira sat on a faded sofa. The vase on the table had paper flowers. There was a picture of Ma Santoshi on the wall. The other wall had the picture of a religious figure. It was Honuman or the monkey God. Another wall had the photo of Sai Baba. Shudha brought the tub. "Oh my!" Two reddish-green roses bloomed. There were three more buds in that plant. Mira hugged Shudha ecstatically and said-"Thank you so, so much Shudha". Shudha did not take the cost of the plant and said-"You don't have to pay me." Mira insisted on taking the amount, but Shudha did not listen to her. After a while, Shudha brought Bhujia and tea on a tray and offered to Mira, "Please". Bhujia was homemade. Shudha had arthritic pain in her leg. She plopped her feet while walking. "Mira, you don't work anymore now, right?"

"No, I don't work. But there are so many things to do at home. You know I am really busy"

Shudha's husband was not at home. He did not have to go to work today and went to the doctor. He had chest pain and a weak heart. Informed Shudha, "He is not well. What can the doctors do? Alcohol and cigarettes have damaged his lungs and heart." After the long story of her husband's illness, Shudha changed the topic. Both of them reminisced the days of the cloth store where they worked together. Shudha enjoyed talking about those memories. They used to work together in the same shop, and then Mira had the government civil service job. She had to attend an examination for it. And Sudha started to work as a factory worker in Charlton.

Shudha gets 500 pounds every month by giving a part of her house on rent. She said to Mira, "There are only two of you in the house. Why don't you give one of your rooms to rent? You will get about the same amount I get. As Greenwich University is near this area, many of the students look for the places to stay." Mira replied, "My son and daughter come and stay with me sometimes. I should not give any room on rent." The house had her own study room, a lot of books, maybe Shudha would not understand all of these. Mira did not proceed with the talk about "renting a room" anymore. Shudha had not studied much. Even after staying in this country for 40 years, she had a hard time speaking in English. Shudha was pretty different than Mira. Still, she was very happy because of the rose. She invited Shudha- "Please do drop by my place someday, Shudha. I'll show you my rose garden." Shudha replied- "Of course, why not? I'll definitely come." Mira took leave from Shudha and came back home. Shudha reassured standing on the door -"Soon I pay you a visit."

Horidas was sleeping. The television was still on. Mira turned it off. Then she went to her garden. It was cloudy now, a drop or two were falling from the sky. Mira thought of planting the green rose plant right away. In between Asad and Bindia. She dug the soil with a shovel and put a layer of fertilised soil. Then she took the plant out of the tub and placed it in the ground. Asad's yellow flower was shining brightly like a big moon. Bindia was her eldest sister's daughter who lived in New Jersey. Bindia was a bit dull, maybe in a few days, it will grow beautiful with the touch of Miracle Gro. Mira kept the tub with the rubbish. Now she would take all of the rubbish to the bin outside. The new reddish-green rose plant was smiling in between Asad and Bindia. Mira looked at the colour of the new rose and wondered, "Can roses be so beautiful?" A few raindrops gathered on yellow Asad. The big petals of the flowers bathed in the raindrops and floated in the air. There was no big drops on Bindia.

Walking through the study room, spare bedroom, she would now go to her own bedroom. She would make a phone call or two . One of the calls would be to Bindia. How was she doing? Why her rose plant named Bindia looked so pale? Was there a connection between the two Bindias? Rose plant Bindia and real-life Bindia? Was Bindia in any kind of trouble? A worry about Bindia was bugging her. She still remembered the day when 25 white roses bloomed on Barkha. On that day, Barkha got a good job. It happened in last month, June. Today was July. May, June, July, August, September, October were the months when roses bloomed to the brim. Then in November, the plants got trimmed for the next year. She usually remained busy in those days with a sharp trimmer and other garden tools. Now there would be flowers for the next four months. When the flowers would not be there, Mira would be feeling a bit sad. Then, she would feel happy after a while and be busy with reading books and other works or probably jot down bits and pieces. Maybe she would go to the theatre or to national portrait gallery to look at pictures old and new. And stand in front of the portrait titled "The Poet". Mira did not know what was in that painting, but she could not remove her eyes from it. Many other paintings grabbed her attention. The thought of why she could not draw herself also came into her mind quite a few times. Though she was a student of literature, she could not write poems, or stories. But sometimes she wrote a few pages' letters to the people who would appreciate them. Some literary flavours seemed in it and hidden emotions. She often felt sad that in the era of mobile phones and emails, no one was interested in writing letters.

Mira now listened to the news from the two-band radio under the umbrella. Recession had affected the whole country badly. Only God knew what would happen. It was relieving for her to think that both Barkha and Abinash were still working. Her daughter looked after the accounts of an office and son remained busy with various responsibilities of a big firm. Both of them were self-sufficient, so there was nothing to worry about. The only difference was that none of them thought about life as Mira did. They would not have a house, garden, husband and kids in their lives. They would stay in the apartments and order takeaways. They would be busy with laptops and sports cars and live together with someone but would not get married. If they did not like the person, they would break up. Having kids? That was a horror for them. None of them would like to get into the trouble of raising kids. Maybe that is the reason why the number of populations had started to decrease in Europe. What would she gain by thinking of these matters, son and daughter's future? Even if she thought about it, they would not change their philosophy of life would not be a different one. No question at all! But a mum's job to think those and Mira was not an exception. The moment she had entered the house with the two-band radio, she noticed that Haridas just woke up. It was his tea time with some biscuits. Or some fruit cake or fairy cake. Mira Sayal turned on the kettle of the kitchen.

Right on 2nd August, Shudha came to visit Mira's place. The garden was in full bloom. Two months had gone by. The apple tree had apples. Some of them were hanging on the tree while Mira plucked some for apple *chutney*. After that, she had not plucked anymore. Bindia had large roses. Abinash did not have many flowers. A few days back, 13 flowers bloomed together on Abinash. Now it was standing quietly. No, Bindia did not have any bad news when the plant Bindia looked dull to her. Such changes in number and quality of the flowers did not bother her much. It was a misconception of her mind perhaps.

Shudha had called her before coming. Shudha's flower plant had six flowers and a bud She had named this plant Shudhamoyi. She liked having this rare plant in her garden. After receiving the plant, they had met only once. Shudha was running to the hospital for her husband then. He had gone through a big cardiac operation. What happened after that was not known to Mira. Here, people did not even know any news of next door, let alone Shudha's news, who lived in 30 minutes' walk away. Shudha did not say anything on phone, but her voice seemed gloomy. Mira also did not ask about her husband. Mira took a bit of special care of the plants because of Sudha. She sprayed some water on them and pulled out some rotten leaves and swept up nicely. She cleaned the two chairs under the umbrella. Shudha was coming around 4 o'clock in the afternoon. Now the day had become shorter. Everyone's opinion - It was an Indian Summer.

Apples were hanging in the apple tree. Horidas asked-"Who's coming?"

"Shudha, Shudha Patel. We used to work together, years back".

"Why is she coming?"

"Just to see me".

"She hadn't come all these years!"

Mira Sayal went to the kitchen. It was not necessary to answer every question. She fried some snacks. They could go to the garden and have them with tea.

Shuda arrived after 7 pm. She was stuck with some important work. She was wearing a light blue dress with red flower prints. On her waist coat she had a peacock. Her hair was fluffed. She had thick hair and did not need any wig like Mira. But it looks less as she oiled it flat most of the time. Now her hair was shampooed and fluffed up. Shudha said-"This waistcoat belongs to my daughter Padma. She threw it away and I've picked it up to wear."

"Oh Really? That's why I was wondering, I haven't seen these before." Shudha's toes with red Kumkum marks were peeping from the two strings of her sandals. Today, everything about Shudha was different. Asked Mira-"How's your husband Ghonosham Patel doing?"

"It is around a month or so that he has been living in a care home."

"Oh, that's sad indeed"

"Daru and ciggies, I mean alcohol and cigarettes. I'd shared with you earlier. All his life he was into these things. After we've bought the house, I have given it on rent. It was tough when our kids lived with us . Now they have left and now on their own. They are the ones to put him in the care home. He needs 24/7 care now. His pension goes to the expense of the home. "

"How long has he been sick?"

"He was sick off and on for twenty years now." Shudha looked at the garden. "Oh my! Isn't that my rose plant? The greenish red rose Padma had selected. Wow! It has flowers as well!" She went near the rose plant. Ghonosham would last only for a month or so perhaps. But Shudha's appearance did not say anything like that. Everything about her was new. Her swollen legs had reduced a bit as well. Shudha looked at the flower plant. Mira informed her that the plant was named after her "Shudhamoyi." Shudha was pleased to know that.

The two women sat under the umbrella. Evening was settling in, the solar lamps of the garden lit up. Horidas did not have dinner before 10pm. Mira Sayal kept chatting freely with Shudha. She said to Shudha, "Ghonosham, I mean your husband's news made me sad."

"There's nothing to be sad about! He has tattered his own lungs with daru and ciggies. He damaged his heart. Has he ever thought of me?" Mira Sayal thought of Horidas. Was there any difference between Ghonosham and Horidas? Only his own diseases and food. But still, when she wrapped up everything and went upstairs, Horidas kissed once or twice on her cheeks. He said- "Goodnight. Sweet dreams Mira." Mira either read a book or listened to music in her room and fell asleep.

It was much late at night while Shudha and Mira talked to each other. The solar light was almost like the moonlight. That's why every garden has solar lamps nowadays. A very heartwarming tune was playing on the FM station. Shudha asked-"I've sponsored and brought him into this country."

"Him? Who?"

"Listen, Mira my *yaar*. Five years back, I met this guy in my country. He is around 50 or 52. He is a widower and has a son who lives abroad. I liked him at the first meeting. No daru or ciggie. A very good human being. I sponsored him here to stay with me." Shuda did spread her arms like peacock's feathers. A peacocks under the clouds waiting to dance in rain.

"Life is very short." Sudha uttered.

"Will he live with you?"

"Who else will he stay with other than me? I brought him here to accompany me."

"Do you want to get married to him?"

"No. We will live together like Padma."

"What will other people say?

"People? Who cares?"

Mira Sayal looked at Shudha Patel's face with surprise. Is this the same Shudha with the pictures of Ma Santoshi, Sai Baba and Hanuman on different walls? There was an amulet around her neck. She remembered that once at their office a Muslim colleague named Khairun had touched Shudha's lunch box. Shudha did not have her lunch that day. She told Mira, "Khairun has touched it. Now I can't have that lunch."

"Why not"- asked Mira.

" I abide by my religion"

That day, Mira did not give a long lecture to Shudha, but she was very surprised why Shudha believed in touchable and untouchable even after living in London for so many years. Shudha used to take bath before completing her morning *puja,* supplications every morning. Shudha is someone who did not study much and lived with all these superstitions.

"You see Mira, I was thinking about my life. What did I get in my whole life? Nothing. After giving two kids, Ghonosham didn't give me anything more. I've earned money all my life. It was the same in my country as well. Moreover, he will pass away soon, there is no way to hold him back. I'm planning ahead for my remaining years. The life I always wanted.

Mira Sayal looked at the garden. Mira looked at the big yellow rose that was still fresh on Asad plant. The solar lights in plants seemed mysterious.. Barkha did not have any flower. A light tune was playing on still by the classic FM. Shudha continued, "Life is somewhat enjoyable now. I've been in the country for so long. Let me be like them for a while. Live together! Why not!."

"If Khairun touches your lunch box now, will you eat from that box? You won't throw it in the bin?"

"Hell no! That is something else.

"That means you won't eat?"

"Kabhi nehi, never. I am a Hindu."

"Oh!" Mira did not like her opinion. She said- "You haven't changed much. Only—"

"I only know that I have to live. I want to live many more years to come. Pradeep is a good man. He has a good physique." She raised her hands above her head as if she was hoping to touch the sky, and her body seemed very stout and youthful. She took out a mirror and put lipstick on. She retouched with her puff on the cheeks and said- "What you are thinking of me, I don't know. But I'm desperate. I love to live anyhow, not waiting to die and hoping to go to paradise. Prodeep once told me - "We live just once."

Mira Sayal did not say anything. She just said-"Maybe you are right Shudha. Sometimes we should think about what we really have in our whole lives."

"You're an educated woman, your situation is different. I used to work in a sawmill in my country. When I came here, I did various odd jobs to run my family. Sweeper, cleaner and what not. The job that I did with you was the best job I've ever had. Now I get pension, I am 67 years old. Let's say and hope if I live ten more years or so, I want to live my life the way I like. Just for once I want to be really happy Mira. Is there any harm in it?"

What could Mira say at this point? The woman whose husband was about to die soon, she had begun her life anew. What advice should she give her? Uff! Why would she even do that? If Shudha did not want to be like her next door neighbour Rosemary, that was her own choice. It was her life - Mira realised it well and that is why did not want to advise her. or give a long lecture on morality. Just very softly uttered -"Have a happy and enjoyable life Sudha." Sudhas eyes seemed misty.

Shudha went away after a while. Horidas had his dinner. Mira Sayal looked at the garden from her window. The flowers of the garden could be seen. It was looking heavenly under the solar lamps. 13, 14, 15 and as she stepped into 16, they had to leave Dehradun. Asad Hashmi's father was a doctor. Asad was perhaps 20 then at best. That lovely young man who juggled oranges or balls with his hands. He used to play various tunes on his mouth organ. Mira Sayal was looking at the garden and thinking about him.

Asad was fighting for life in one of the Nursing homes in California. It was the last stage of cancer. His two wives have left him one after another. Many other women came into his life. But still he remembered Mira's face. Mira Malhotra. She used to look at his juggle with her huge eyes and open mouth. Long braided hair on her chest. 13, 14, 15 and the moment she stepped into 16, they had to leave Dehradun. She did not give time for him to express a special feeling that he had for her. He would have said it to her either today or tomorrow. Then? Who knows what would have happened after that? If he somehow he knew that a rose plant in Mira's back garden was named Asad, would have been able to breathe his last with a strange happiness. But everyone was not that lucky in this world to know such a news. A rose plant named Asad was glowing in the garden. Mira could not forget him even now. If Asad Hasmi was 72 now, Mira was 67. But he remembered the school-going Mira with braids hair with red flowers. Pretty Mira who used to giggle in everything and opened her mouth wide with surprise to see him juggling. Her huge eyes were painted with Kajal. And a tiny Bindia.

Mira Sayal woke up in the morning. She had a habit of Pranayama. She would sit on the garden chair. In the winter, she sat inside the house and in summer, she preferred outside. She had fallen asleep while reading a book last night. Mira had dreamt a haphazard dream. Such a nuisance! Such a dream at her age? She saw that someone hugged her and was kissing her passionately for a long time. Shudha! She is the cause of such a dream, said Mira to herself. Her discussion on such topics brought all these dreams. Mira washed her face with soapy water well in the morning and came to the garden. She looked at the wall of the garden where different birds came to rest. A blackish-red bird was sitting on the wall. Reddish feathers with white legs. It was a different one. Where did the bird come from? Previously, other types of the birds came to perch on the wall. During the last Eid day in Dehradun, Asad Hasmi had worn a gorgeous Punjabi. The colour of the punjabi was blackish-red, with some yellow needle work on the chest. The pyjama was white. Not really a *chost* pyjama, but somewhere between a *chost* and a lose pyjama. His body emitted fragrance of *attar*. He had *surma* on his eyes, dressed up for Eid. Mira looked at him mesmerised, "You're looking great. Really lovely."

"Really?" -Said Asad. He played the tune of *Aye Mere Dil kehi our chal*-"My heart lets go somewhere else."- Then turning back a radiant smile for Mira.

The bird on the wall had reddish-black chest with yellow spots here and there, white legs..

Translated by Sabreena Ahmed

Dr Bina Biswas

Of Biryani and Hyder Ali

Hyder Ali looked visibly demoralised on a typical Friday afternoon during the holy month of fasting. As it was, after a week's hard work, he always expected biryani on his plate after returning from the mosque offering his evening prayers.

His favourite beef biryani was missing from his lunch menu today. They had banned all meat, including beef, this time. He looked at his youngest son, who seemed to have settled down well with the chicken and the governance system. He took an exasperated sidelong glance at his begum before pushing the platter away. There was an unexpressed gloom in the house.

Hyder had always kept his thoughts about his nation and gastronomical delights separate. On the one hand, he tried very hard to remain patriotic, and on the other, he did not know what his nation got to do with the beef. This time, it was getting complicated, and his culinary fits of appetite refused to give way despite his best toils.

He tried to keep it hidden, but at times like this, he felt helpless. Probably, the Ramadan fasts became meaningless for him if he did not get to eat beef biryani during the *iftar*.

He was a carpenter by profession and lived in a three-storey house in a congested locality in the heart of the city of Meerut. He had his eldest son continue his woodcraft legacy and now spent most of his time praying and eating. He heard something about this *ban* at the market and thought it to be a rumour. But when the much-craved delicacy went missing on his plate, he did not know what to do. He was the last person on the earth to get angry, and nothing could provoke him to utter one or two expletives for those who banned the beef. He closed his eyes and tried to gulp down the pangs of hunger along with exasperation he felt towards the entire issue.

Hyder did not recollect having eaten anything other than the beef biryani during the Ramadan evenings while breaking the fast. The other meats on the menu had never tempted him. The spread was always quite elaborate, and his begum always took great care to make everything delectable.

Retiring to his bed on the rooftop under the vast dark sky with some diehard twinkling stars, Hyder waited for his begum to come and massage his legs. After all, he had fasted the whole day and could not even get to eat his favourite biryani; he deserved all the pampering.

A familiar smell of stale fat wafting out from nowhere, riding the hot wind, reached Hyder's nose. His olfactory senses immediately became alert. The sweet noise of banter and soft suppressed laughter filled the air as Hyder drifted to sleep on his cot...

... Hyder, dressed as an Afghan Prince, sat on something like a monarchial bed. The place resonated with celestial music, and women wearing expensive silk dresses danced before him. He felt like the Sahenshah Akbar sitting in his harem. Music, exotic food, expensive china sets, and huge platters full of his favourite biryani...

Suddenly he felt a nudge and came back to the present from his dream world, and there was his begum standing in attendance to offer her services as the masseuse. Shabnam begum perched herself next to Hyder, urging him to move and give her space. Her hips were enormous, and the protruding belly had made her breasts appear small. She always kept her torso covered with her *dupatta* to save herself from the lustful eyes of imaginary men. Imaginary because she stayed indoors and mainly in the Zenana, where only male family members were allowed to venture in. Now, the robes engulfed her body, obscuring her silhouette and increasing her sense of personal shame.

Hyder had married her when she was eighteen and a major as per the law. She bore six children quickly, lost her youth and vigor to childbirth, and slowly gained weight. Sex had become a periodic affair with Hyder. Every other night when he mounted Shabnam as a habit, he would feel frustrated and swear and dismount, wetting her inner. He missed the intimacy and passion he had once shared with his wife. On the other hand, Shabnam would deem herself worthy of Hyder's love and try to feel gratified without even experiencing the peak.

Hyder was now beside himself in grief. He would not get his beef biryani during this holy month of fasting. Beef or chicken, both mattered to him, but the sacred memories of the deep-fried spices and the long-grained rice with chunks of marinated meat pieces kept troubling him.

He hardly went out to the alleys that reeked intolerable stench from the gutters. He was trying to identify the smells that wreaked havoc in those lanes. He diverted all his attention to identify and distinguish the aroma of chicken and beef. He felt the entire universe had conspired against him, including the present ruling tyrants.

The whole story of the buffalo was too obvious to explain to Hyder. He wanted only *Bade ka gosht*, beef, like a wayward child, and it had been banned. Hyder was in an extreme dilemma. Though he loved his beef, he first had a beef to pick with the government. He had grown up eating his favourite meat, and no one ever had any objection. Since his birth, he had lived in this city, and his *abbu* was also born here. His country was the same, and his area was the same, but suddenly they deprived him of eating his favourite dish. It went beyond his comprehension. He wondered, what right did someone have to stop the beef in his biryani plate?

Sitting forsaken on the culvert on the stinky gutter, Hyder overheard that the government was about to limit the family size. The loudspeakers atop the mosques would go too. He was past his procreating age, but he loved seeing more and more children around him. Poor Hyder, he did not know what for was it? The muezzin's call always worked like his clock around the day. How did it come in the way of someone? Hyder rose to his feet and went hurriedly towards his house. He had to alert his begum about all these and lament his appetite loss.

Hyder felt sad looking at his beef-biryani-deprived kids and heaved a deep sigh. It was hard for him to imagine a beef-less biryani during the festival. The more he exercised his brain over this, the more fatigue consumed his mind.

Hyder was a reasonable man, but this ban seemed impossible to reason
with these days. With no hope of a resolution in sight, he just wanted to get as much sleep as possible. With a fully packed fasting month ahead, Hyder needed his rest. Keenly aware that his begum worked equally hard to raise their family at home every day, he closed his eyes and wished for a respite for her.

There was a procession on the road. Hyder ran out of his house to the road to see what it was. There were lights and fireworks amid low volume *kirtans* playing on the speakers. Some men and boys wearing masks of the Monkey-God and dressed like monkeys walked past, celebrating *Hanuman Jayanti*. Like every year, this year too, Hyder had rushed out of the house to have a good look at the spectacle. But, in his heart of hearts, he missed his beef biryani.

Suddenly, as if woken up from his reverie, Hyder saw his neighbour Mr. Gupta thrusting something in his hands.

What is it?

Hyder was surprised. It was rare for his Hindu neighbour to bring him something.

Hyder looked puzzled.

Got this for you. Happy Hanuman Jayanti.

The songs from the procession now seemed distant. Hyder stood amused, holding the sweet box in his hand.

This time he felt Ramadan had some other flavours to offer, too. He went indoors and distributed the sweets to his family members and helped himself with some two or three *laddoos.*

Mojaffor Hossain

A Trip Down Memory Lane

"Imagine, you want to become someone special, but you know it is next to impossible for you to carry through on your ambition. Then again, you don't want to be anyone other than the person you are bent on becoming." A few days before his death, the old man had told me: "You know, death means self-destruction." He was of such an age that he would have naturally met his end, had he waited for a couple of days more. Despite his age and infirmity, he took the decision. Earlier, he had meaningfully gestured to me about what he would do. As I wasn't sharp enough, I couldn't fathom out the depth of what he had tried to convey.

"Before my death, I'd like to take a decision all by myself at least. It wouldn't be a decision of my family, neither would it be a choice of the society, state or my destiny - nothing and nobody would be able to put me off from taking my option. It would be absolutely my decision." After footing the bill for his tea last day, he said these words while putting an effort to straighten up his unsteady body.

A little distance away from the makeshift tea-stall, situated in front of a shrine and perched atop bamboos on the bank of the Padma River, we would sit side by side every Friday and Saturday. Day after day passed by, and we suddenly discovered that we kept seated, next to each other, at the same place from evening to night till the teashop remained open. Simply presuming that a new person was having his seat beside me every day, I avoided him not being interested in knowing him. So did he. I wouldn't have thought about it had the tea-seller not asked me about that person that day: "Why is Chacha not around these days? He didn't come last week as well."

"Which Chacha are you talking about?" Assuming that the shopkeeper was making a mistake, I asked him a counter question as a matter-of-factly.

"Don't you remember the person who sits beside you every day? You guys take tea together, and when it is time for the shop to be closed, you guys leave this place, paying your respective bills."

When he came and sat beside me the next day, I did the icebreaking. Hardly could I figure out the number of days I had spent sitting alongside him since we started our conversation that day.

"Were you sick?" Briefly, I asked.

Expressing reluctance, he said: "Don't know why!" He sounded curt, saying nothing about why he didn't come. I didn't have any special curiosity, either. We kept seated as we used to, with no words exchanged between us for quite some time. As minutes were ticking away, again I asked him in a single sentence: "Do you come and sit here every day?"

"I love sitting down beside a river." After he had his sight immersed in the river, he verbalised something like that. As he mumbled, I couldn't catch everything of what he had said.

"I come here on Fridays and Saturdays. I have been coming here for four years. Unless I get caught up in important work, I don't miss out on this opportunity." I gave a brief rundown of my interest.

"Oh!" Oscillating his mouth for some time, he could produce that much in recognition to what I had said. Since then, we used to exchange one or two sentences between us almost every day.

"I write. Rivers inspire me. In fact, they don't, what you could say is that I bring out the best from it. It could be because I grew up having seen lots of ponds during my childhood. After leaving this place, I go home and play music, particularly Tagore songs or Robishankar's sitar on my device till I fall asleep. If I don't do it, I just can't write a single sentence. This has become a bad habit now." On my own volition, I told him about me and my passion on a Friday. If I were to talk about my writing, I would say it wasn't worth mentioning. However, I had to tell him about it as I was required to say something appropriate. Actually, I wanted to know why he kept seated at that place for such a long time. He didn't tell me anything that day. Listening to what I had said, he panned his face only once to have a close look at me. It was a Saturday next day, and he came up with a reply: "I just sit down, no specific reason as such." Pausing for a few moments, he again said: "In this place, the river is quite sedate." Thereafter, he didn't say anything else. Neither did I request him anymore. The reason I loved coming here was to sit down in absorbing silence. I didn't want to get enmeshed in random talks, deviating myself from my purpose of being here. However, we would sporadically talk daily. One day, he said: "The place is well-lit always. I hate being in darkness."

"Do I come here and sit down for the same reason?" I soliloquised. When someone is without any job, he or she is usually deluged by stray thoughts. When thought after thought keeps rushing in and gets used up at some point, one is left with no choice but to keep sitting down, with a blank mind. After a long time, I wanted to think out why I kept sitting down at the same place. It could be that the teaseller was right in putting adequate amount of sugar in tea, not less or more. Barely could I remember any shop in the city where I drank such a perfect and regular sugar-tea combination. Or there could be a relationship between the banyan tree we would sit under, and the banyan tree situated at the roundabout in front of my village home. While lazing about on the seat, I tried to establish a connection between the two.

After my father had left for the village market for business purposes, I would lie down alone on a bamboo-made resting platform under the banyan tree, near my home. If I had stayed at home, my stepmother would be causing suffering to me, bringing on matters of no importance: she would be twisting a lock of my hair around her fingers, or she would be cracking jute stalks, gathered together beside the *chula* (an earthen cooker), across my back, one after another. Making a sense of what had been going on, one day my father had told Mojjel chacha: "Give him a haircut like a *kodom* (a local variety of flower)." I refused to do so because I had thought that the pain, caused by the twisting of my hair, would be comparatively less compared to the torture I had been handed out through jute-stalk thrashing. By any chance, if she had found bamboo rattan or Babla (a sort of a thorny tree from which gum is obtained) twigs nearby, she would be grabbing them to beat me up in ferocious aggressiveness. Presuming that she would be flogging harder at my back if my hair had been shortened, Mojjel chacha spared me from further injury by not giving me a haircut. Looking back at those days today, I could fathom out the reason why he didn't let me have the haircut. Mila and I were immediately succeeding each other in birth. Since I was motherless, that family had been taking extra care of me. I heard that I had been breastfed by Mila's mother. From that perspective, this youngest grandmother could be called my milk-mother. As Fozu-dada, Mila's father, had not been in the country, we could take advantage of many things. Although I didn't see him, I had heard a lot about him. With the growth of my understanding of things, I came to know that Fozu-dada (grandpa) had gone abroad for work. I didn't know whether or not he had returned to the country. I could be interested in knowing about him had Mila been alive.

In the name of leaving me in grandma's care, my father had been taking her out for some minutes, keeping Mila and I in a room. After a few minutes, chick-like grunts would be coming out from the darkness of the straw-cutting room, situated right behind the chamber we had been locked in. Those short guttural sounds had been the end-result of the pleasure-pain sensations of their sexual delight. Mila and I had followed them one day and saw them having sex. On return to the house, Mila had said: "It is pretty much gratifying! Would you like to play a game like that? It had been all silence that took us over. Being naked, we had remained locked in embrace for some time and gone asleep. After the incident had happened, there was an occurrence some days later: that day the youngest grandma together with my father had seen us sleeping together being naked and interlocked. Since that incident, I had been barred from going to Mila's house. I had been made to sleep on the veranda outside the room of my father and stepmother. Their stifled war of words had woken me up that night.

"Did you hear me? Why don't you lift your clothes up?" Baba had sounded irritably impatient.

"I am not physically well today. Can't you stop doing it today?" Pleadingly, the stepmother had said.

It had been a habit of my irascible father to go raving mad at simple things. I could understand that he had taken the door-latch in his hand.

"Do you want me to push it in? You fucking woman, don't you have any other time to give this excuse of illness?" After he had hit her twice with the door-latch, he left home in a fit of pique and went straight to Mila's house leaping over the boundary wall, cutting the distance short.

Coming out of the door, the stepmother had started kicking me left and right, without any reasons. "*Haramzada,* get up and go out of my sight!" She had said, letting her steam off. Whenever I would come into view of the childless stepmother, she would lunge at me with hardened reactions, being aware of her child-bearing incapacity. After I had left the place, I entered the room of the farm- labourer's raised bamboo-frame platform, situated in the compound outside the goat-shed, and I kept myself seated there. Probably, two hours had gone by, and my father came back home, jumping over the same wall. After he had a wash-up of his hands and face with the tube-well water, he went into the room, took something from there and went away, putting those things on his shoulder.

In the morning, Mila's blood-stained body had been recovered from the elevated scaffold, placed under the banyan tree. She had been found dead, and my father had gone traceless. Then my stepmother and I had parted our ways. I had my secondary-level schooling started from my maternal uncle's home. Since that occurrence, I had gone to my village only once. On hearing that the youngest grandma had gone insane, I went to see her. On that occasion, the effort of cloaking the truth of my mother's death in a shroud of secrecy had been brought to my notice. Also, I had come to know about Mila's other identity. As because the youngest grandma had lost her mental balance, some villagers wanted me to believe that whatever she had told me had been utterly nonsensical. Based on the hearsay that Mila's ghost had been giving the locals harrowing experiences at night, the bamboo-platform under the banyan tree was broken down. Although I had a wish to spend a night out there once, I could not. I never had any belief in ghostlike images of any person. Being scared, I think I had started to believe in it. After I had come to know about the apparition of Mila's dead body being manifested to the living, I became frightened, too. I had become terrified not because I remembered our bed scene, but for other reason: perhaps, I would be able to know about it some days later. Surely, I would. Perhaps, someday Mila would suddenly come down from the banyan tree to the ground to tell me the reason. Or it could be that I would never know the reason.

As my companion kept seated silently, I could think about many things related to my past and future.

"Our river was exactly like this." Breaking the silence, the old man said, adding: "Gradually, the courtyard was extended only to be lost into the river. I heard that my mother gave me birth while she was cleaning dishes in the river-water."

"Which river?" Once I thought of asking him the question, but I didn't interrupt as I found him talking under his breath.

"My father was the owner of a wholesale fish depot. It was a huge business. During the 1946 Bihar riot, the violent mob stabbed him, piercing him through. Thereafter, he was thrown into the stream of the river Koshi. Taking great pains, my grandma would intently sit at the bank of the river to draw up air to detect his son's body-smell until she herself was swept out into the river one day."

"Did you come here from across the border after that incident?" I queried.

"Yes? Did you tell me anything? The wind is repressively unmoving. There could be a storm! Would you like to get up?" The old man made an effort to stand up from the bamboo-made seat and trudged wearily along the riverbank, dragging his left leg. This was the route he used to use to come to this place and go back.

Last night's storm left a branch of the banyan tree broken, making the whole tree looking windswept. Caught in a dust-storm once, Mila had her droopy shoulder-long hair tangled up like that. Sliding down her feet into the water of a pond, she hadn't been able to unscramble the terrible mix-up, despite her efforts. Pretending goodness, I had affixed some Chorakata (a kind of prickly thistle that sticks fast to the clothes) to her hair in the guise of coming to her aid. After she had burst into a prolonged high-pitched cry, the youngest grandma rushed to the spot and showered down fisticuffs on my back. She had been ceaselessly crying. I can't remember today as to why I had idiotically laughed that day, seeing her snivelling.

Today, the old man came earlier than me. The teashop was yet to open. The storm had swept away the shop's thatched roof; it could take two days to put it back together. We felt we were being increasingly consumed by a strong desire to drink tea.

"Would you like to go for a walk?" The old man enquiringly asked. I helped him to stand up by holding one of his rib bones. We kept walking along the riverside.

"A lot of Muslims had gone to Pakistan due to the Bihar riot. Why did you come here? Their language was Urdu. But you speak Bangla so well." I asked him.

"My mother was a Bangali. She was from Kushtia. My father had worked at the Mohini mill for some time. On his own choice, he had married her then. After my mother's family members had received the death news of my father, my youngest maternal chacha (uncle) went to Kushtia to bring us back."

There were no teashops in and around the place. We kept on walking. I couldn't remember when I held on to one of his hands. While walking, I recalled the days I had with my father. Of course, I wouldn't like to cast my mind back to that person who had fathered me: he was that father who had pressed down a pillow on my mother's mouth one night, and then he had hanged her, tightening the grip of her sari against the door's crossbeam. Her crime was that she could know about the identity of Mila's real father. Actually, Mila's mother was my father's youngest chachi (aunt). They didn't want the matter to go public. Fozu chacha had been on his way to Italy then. While crossing the Libyan part of the blue Mediterranean, he had made the last phone-call. Thereafter, there had been no news about him. As Mila had become a victim of rape and murder to her lewd progenitor, I wouldn't like to hark back to the physical existence of my flesh and blood father. Truly, I would like to think of a rarefied being called father - the story of a feeling I remained deprived of all through my life.

"My father was washed away by the Koshi, and my mother was swept out to the Padma. I don't know whether it happened when they were alive or dead. My mother had to struggle a lot to save herself during the Bihar riot to return to the country. During an inky darkness of a night in 1971, the Pakistani barbaric troopers had thrown her into the fiercely flowing Padma water. After they had fired a bullet at my leg, they left the spot. However, I had wanted them to fire the shot at my head. I had shouted out to them for firing another bullet, but they didn't pay any heed to it." The old man was huffing and puffing while narrating the incident.

"You need to have some rest. Shall we sit here?" I asked him, clutching his hand even harder. Meanwhile, the night became impenetrably thicker. Also, we forgot about our hunt for tea.

"Would you mind taking me to a lighted place? I just can't tolerate darkness." The old man said.

In search of light, we walked up some more distance.

"Did you want to be somebody who is just impossible to become?" I asked him.

"What do you mean? Never did I want to become someone special! By becoming nothing or nobody, I wish I could go back to my past. I always cherished that dream. I have remained alive only to go back to the juncture of two historical ages." He spoke sotto voce.

"What's the point of thinking like this? You didn't have a hand in the twists and turns of history. Whatever is written in history today wouldn't change at all, even if you could go back to that historical period."

"That is the end-all of the collective history, but there is something called a personal history. I could put an end to myself at that historical juncture. Could you tell me what I got after living a dream for life for so long, eventually? Barely could I decipher what he tried to say. He spoke so indistinctly. "In certain activities and times, the significance of living life is not always the solution. For that reason, you have to understand when you have to come to a halt," he added.

Many a time, the path gives us an impetus to make a move on to create a route for itself. Being dictated by his or her mind, is it possible for a traveller to steer him or her in the right direction? I have remained rooted to the spot where I have been. Opening my eyes wide open, I find that I have come a long way from my past. A thought like this consumes me.

The teashop opened a week after. When the old man came there limping, the Maghreb prayer-call was coming out from the shrine's mosque. I sat down on the bamboo-made stool, clasping his hand. I could feel that his body was trembling.

"You need rest. You shouldn't have come here today." I said compassionately. Rest was silence: it was as if we kept sitting there as a subject of an artist's painting of an eroded river, with two have-nots sitting next to each other along the riverbank. Perhaps we were served with hot teas many a time; perhaps there wasn't any tea coming our way. It could be that we sipped at tea, or it might be that we didn't drink tea at all. In quietude, we kept seated stone-still for a long time against the backdrop of the zephyr-generated wavelet of the flowing water, the evanescent reverberations of the Banyan tree-leaves touching each other, the sound of the loud recitation of Allah's name emanating from the shrine, the chitter-chatter of a few people surrounding their domestic issues emerging from other side of the tea-stall, the unmelodious tune of a flute coming out from afar and the never-ending loquacity of the rickshawallas emitting from behind us.

"Before my death, I would like to take one decision at least..." After that he gave utterance to what he wanted to say and trudged away, dragging his leg.

"We take all our personal decisions independently, but do they remain exclusive?" I replied to myself without comprehending what he actually meant.

Gradually, the river became blurry and the path he plodded through. Slowly, the tea-stall went out of my view as well. As the night became impassably dense, the rippling sound streaming down the river, the repeating chants of Allah's name coming out of the shrine and the beam of light spreading from the lamppost started to get diffused into memories, keeping me as a witness. Only the banyan tree stood face to face, giving rise to my ability to have the powers of retention

Translated by Haroonuzzaman

Leila Samarrai

Vodka, 'The Adventures of Boris K.'

In his tiny two-by-two hole in the wall, Boris K. sat with a dignified expression on his face and his legs out in a straddle. He wore two left slippers of diverse colours. As he casually turned to peer in the cracked mirror, he was greatly displeased by the sight of his slicked-back grey hair. He attempted to part it à la Sieg Heil but could not really pull it off because – he wore a flower in his hair, you see.

At springtime, as the locks of his raven hair started blooming, he left all the women breathless (left-wing ones in particular, as they were especially partial to flowers).

"There is a certain symbolism to them," they claimed.

Boris K. was a seasoned communist, a ruin left behind by the transition, a redundant loser. Like many others, he looked back on the times when he subscribed to the Labourer newspaper with nostalgia. It used to be a matter of prestige.

Due to his former high-ranking positions as the coffee brewer and sentry for the Trade Union sessions, he retained the habit of sitting, sleeping and eating while dressed in a grey business suit. On that cold evening, he was waiting for the arrival of his landlady while reading "The Trial". Remembering the times past and the chanting of the famous "Comrade Fidel, if you so said/we'd go live in a car shed," Boris K. mused how, everything said and done, he was actually still living according to his beliefs. The very thought was heartwarming. Boris' "car shed" belonged to none other than the very harpy, the very shrew who announced her intent to arrive at 6 AM on the dot. At that time, with the first rays of sun, she was to materialise in the flat. Boris felt hungry and mildly nauseous. Maybe it was the fear of the landlady, or perhaps an omen of the apocalypse. He felt confused. By the powers of the left-wing, Boris K. was no coward!

He approached the old refrigerator, opened the handless door, and saw a drunken lady squeezed into a small glass cage. It was a bottle of vodka, the Russian standard with 40 per cent of alcohol. The poster on the wall offered him support and encouragement, or at least so it appeared to Boris K. It seemed to be saying "Bottoms up, Boris! Long live the counter-revolution!"

"Alas… if only I could squeeze myself inside just like you," Boris thought wistfully. He envisioned his landlady, the morning sun illuminating her like a halo, menacingly brandishing the electricity bill. He huddled against the wall, crying like a baby, his cheek resting against a poster. A thought pierced his aching head, which throbbed as if clenched within a hoop. "But I don't drink."

"Now or never," he spoke out loud. After the first sip, it occurred to him that he should attempt to seduce his ageing landlady. He was determined to fight to the bitter end.

"This is how Alexander the Great charged against the Persians with his sword!" he thought, detaching his tear-stained cheek from the poster. "Is the casino Alexander still open?" he asked the wall hopefully, his face beaming.

Feverishly, he contemplated the way to get out of debt. Even without a penny to his name, Boris K. decided to try his luck at the adjacent casino. He took a big gulp of vodka and stumbled Toppling the chair, he knocked down the suit and the grey socks and grabbed for the closet. He let the bottle drop out of his hand after the second swig. Somewhere in the pile of jumbled clothing, Boris spotted a formal suit à la Vienna. He looked at it from all sides. He looked both ways furtively, as if he were not alone in the room, so surprised he was at the appearance of a beautiful, shining suit in such a gloomy environment. He stroked the buttons gently with his fingertips. It was exactly what he needed. Boris K. looked up at the ceiling and muttered "Thanks!"

Delighted, he cast another glance toward the closet and noticed the secret barrier dividing it into two parts. He grabbed the handle and shook it tentatively, but it appeared to be locked. Boris K. stepped back and stood in the middle of the room. The bottle of vodka back in his hand, he raged at the locked compartment.

"You're hiding some great treasure, I know it!" "

He heard something rattle in one of the suit pockets. His hands shook as he rifled through the pockets, but all he found there were some brass buttons.

"Pure gold," he soothed himself.

Donning the suit, he decided to use the buttons as gambling tokens. Thrilled with his incredible discovery, Boris K. danced a few bars of the Viennese waltz in front of the cracked mirror, arranging his hair. Out of breath, he fell onto the sofa. He was transported back to

the harsh reality by the picture of Fidel Castro winking –
or so it seemed to Boris K – straight at him.

"Too much to drink," Boris concluded. Pulling himself
together he threw the cheap buttons into the corner of the
room, took one glance at the electricity bill and burst
into tears.

The old lady entered just as she promised – illuminated
by the first rays of the sun. On her dress, tailored back
in the forties, she wore an embroidered swastika.

"The Brazilian tarantula. Such an elegant little animal,"
she explained to the curious butcher's wife in passing.
She wore lace gloves, dirty fingernails showing through.
Smoothing down her oily hair, she swiped a dainty
finger over one of her eyebrows, tattooed according to
the latest fashion. Following the unfortunately drawn
arch, she cast an Ilse-Koch-like look to Boris K. A
cynical smile spilled across her elderly, clenched lips.

"Cash on the table," she pulled out a stopwatch from her
undershirt, "in 60… 59… 58…" As she counted down, it
appeared, the last seconds of Boris K's short life, the age
spots on her cheeks broke through the layers of golden
foundation and bright lipstick on her cheekbones.

"Do sit down, old Fräulein," stammered Boris K,
pointing to the sofa as full of holes as a Swiss cheese and
stinking of cigarettes. The old woman threw him a
contemptuous look. Boris K. realized his mistake.
"Meine Frau,.. I… I… Frau, bitte," he stammered,
hypnotized by the embroidered swastika flanked by a
flashy heart-shaped medallion. Finally, he murmured
"Just let me run to the casino. I forgot my wallet next to
the roulette hero."

"The casino, you say?" The old woman swiped the corners of her widely open mouth using a forefinger and a thumb.

"I swear by… this poster on the wall, Fräulein Suzy!"

She studied him like one would an insect and, with a sudden twist, cast a look filled with loathing at the poster of Fidel Castro. Stalin was her true love, but it was a fact she carefully concealed.

"Too bad he is an infidel," she said as the light pushed its way through the dirty windows, illuminating her head like a halo. Her voice rang with the austerity typical of elderly women of reckless youth, who remembered their days of decadence just a touch too wistfully. Once easy, now a puritan, she had changed the dirty skin of her body and threw it on the altar of martyrdom, akin to a snake.

Boris K. repented his actions. He felt like taking off his nonexistent à la Vienna hat.

The old woman turned, eyes bulging, and approached him at a menacing pace. With the stance of an SS officer, her long nose touching the chest Boris K, Frau sniffed him, noticed the empty bottle of vodka and contemptuously waved her hand. Settling on the sofa, she closed her eyes in the manner of a yogi. It lasted a whole of fifteen minutes, with Boris K. perspiring, dabbing the sweat from his brow and occasionally massaging her feet, until she cried

"Genug! Stop!" Her wide-open eyes startled Boris K and he immediately stood to attention. "At ease!" Boris K. threw the left shoe off his right foot, hips swaying. "I forgive you, just as my Fritz would have done," she murmured wistfully, remembering her old love – a high-ranking SS officer, carried off by the maelstrom of war. Boris K. burst into tears of happiness. "But, under in condition!," she roared in a thunderous voice. Boris K. was all ears. "I will write off your debt if you can squeeze yourself into this bottle." The Frau pointed at the vodka bottle. "Verständlich? Understand?" the implacable Frau screeched.

Boris K. glanced at the bottle, then at his soft, pink hand (he was an artist, and it is well known that they do absolutely nothing under the sun). He wanted to protest, to say that one could not treat the oppressed classes so. Squeezing people into bottles like that? Not even Mengele would have thought of that, he thought – but said nothing. Somehow, he managed to bend his back; he crumpled, growing smaller, lowering his proud fists, his skilful fingers curled, and his head hung low. Thus, his entire body was distorted.

Boris K. kept diminishing before the terrible powers of the frau, finally, growing small enough to squeeze his tiny hand into the vodka bottle, followed by his shoulder, chest and spine – the latter proved easy enough to squeeze into the bottle – and finally his feet, which by that point had completely refused to obey him. Thus Boris K. successfully completed his task under the Frau's contented smile. Only Boris' two large, terrified eyes remained visible.

The giant frau stood up, took the vodka bottle and headed for the locked compartment – the strictly guarded secret of all secrets. For years she was suspected of hiding, if not jewellry, then at least Fritz's letters there. She reached into her pocket for the gilded key and opened the plywood compartment. Frau looked with pride upon the arranged bottles of numerous manufacturers – English and French, but mostly German. One bottle contained Sir Gawain, her former tenant, the second Herr Hans, and the third, Jean-Paul. From the fourth, the Obergruppenführer Fritz (the former supreme commander of the Waffen-SS) smiled at his lover, the Frau, who blew him a tender kiss. Each of the bottles contained a tenant hopefully peering through the stained glass of his prison, every one of them grateful to his landlady for being so very generous as to write off his debt.

Louise Whyburd

Leap of faith

By the side of a flourishing pond sat a frog and a toad on a hot summer's day. In the centre of the pond, there was a lily pad, it was luscious and green with a beautiful white flower that had bloomed above it which created a perfect spot to sit under and cool down in the shade.

It looked very enticing, so the frog leapt across with a one mighty bounce onto the lily pad.

"Come on, join me on here it's lovely and cool" said the frog, the toad looked hesitant and shook his head and turned to hop away.

Confused by the toad's reaction the frog hopped back across on to the bank of the pond and sat beside the toad, the toad gazed down into the pond.

"What's wrong, are your legs not working?" joked the frog

"I don't think I can make it," said the toad.

The frog looked at the toad slightly bemused by his response yet could see despite his joke that the toad didn't react but sat there in silence and looked sad. So, he decided to sit beside him.

"I'll sit beside you until you're ready to leap across, I can't leave you here alone in this heat," said the concerned frog.

Five minutes went by, the toads' eyes were still looking down starring into the pond, he was clearly lost in thought. The frog noticed the toad still looked gloomy, so he asked the toad what was wrong, the toad replied in a quiet almost whispering tone,

"I am too fearful, what if I leap and I do not make it?" At this point the frog sensed the doubt was more than just jumping across onto the lily pad, so he sat alongside the toad looking at the calm pond in silence keeping him company.

It was noon at this point and the sun's rays were beating down even hotter. The toad cleared his throat and turned to the frog with sorrow in his eyes and said,

"Ever since I was a tadpole, all I wanted was love and support, but I was separated from school of tadpoles my mother had spawned, and ever since then I've felt lost in this world and stopped believing in myself."

Now the frog had led a very different life, he had grown up in a pond full of life surrounded by all his siblings, he spent his days swimming around and exploring until he was ready to make it out into the world alone. His memories were filled with joy and support, so it gave him no reason to ever doubt himself.

The frog sat there for a minute contemplating what the toad had just said, he looked at the toad and said with encouragement in his voice,

"Never quit, if you stumble, get back up. Try it and leap across and if you don't make it then try and try again. You can do it; I know you can. I believe in you!"

The toad sat there for a few moments and pondered over what the frog had just said, when his gaze looked up and suddenly before the frog could say anything the toad took one giant leap and landed on the lily pad and sat beneath the shade, he looked back at the frog a remarked in a cheeky tone,

"What's wrong, are your legs not working?"

The frog joined the toad on the lily pad under the shadow of the beautiful white flower looking out over the pond, they sat watching the sun blazing down on the gentle ripples their leaps had just created from landing, when the toad asked the frog,

"You are a stranger, why did you stop to help me for?"

The frog looked at the toad with a smile on his face and said,

"We should plant trees under whose shade we do not plan to sit."

Part Three

Prose Poems

Poems by David Lee Morgan

Killing a dog

I've killed lots of mice and fish and worms, a few rats,
one or two crawdads, no elephants, billions of bacteria,
lots of insects, a few snakes and one dog. The dog, I
didn't kill with my own two hands. I killed her the way
Presidential advisors kill - except I watched up close.

I guess the thing I remember most about Tiger was her
farts. Tiger was half Labrador and half something
bigger, a lot bigger. Labradors are famous for their
smelly farts. Tiger's farts were true Labrador farts, only
bigger, a lot bigger. But Tiger had more than smelly farts
- she had personality

Afterwards they sent us a card - just offering their
sympathy - do doctors do that when they kill humans?

Her favourite farting location was on the kitchen floor.
Sitting with her butthole pressed against the linoleum
enhanced the acoustic dimension enormously. She
would be so startled by the noise that she would leap up,
spin around and try to stare quizzically - and innocently -
into her own asshole. Each time, she was as surprised as
the time before. We could never figure out if she was
that good an actress or that stupid.

When she got old, her back legs wouldn't work right

Right now, I am almost writing this through tears, but if I had it to do all over again, I would still kill her. She was my sisters jailer.

For years and years, Tiger used to protect us - my sister, her son, and any of the rest of us who were around. I think my sister really relied on Tiger's big, safe presence, especially after Tony moved out.

We had succeeded in turning her into a vegetable, but we couldn't kill her. Finally, they got a really long needle - it looked like a railroad spike - and jammed it into her heart.

Tiger was old. She couldn't get up without help. I left the basement door open. I didn't do it on purpose.

I could imagine myself putting down old people in similar circumstances. Maybe it would be easier: dogs don't show their age as much as humans do.

Tiger was missing a toe. It might have been cancer. My sister didn't ask them to look. She didn't want to know - afterwards she was sorry. If we had known for sure that Tiger had cancer it would have been easier.

When I got back, she was hanging upside down. She had fallen, and her rear leg had gotten caught between the stairs and the furnace. Beneath her was a little blood and a pool of saliva - it looked like quarts.

They couldn't find a vein, so they tried over and over. After the first shot, her tongue hung out and lay flat on the table like wet paper.

Charlie Savage

Kings Cross. The kitchen was on the second floor. Charlie Savage destroyed pretty much everything on the inside and then started to work his way out. He broke the windows. Then he tore out the window frame. Most of the wall came with it. Jeanette stood frozen in the middle of the room holding the baby and saying, "Why are you doing this?"

Charlie couldn't answer.

Kreutzberg. Charlie Savage told me about London. It sounded like another planet. He said everything was done by keeping a list. There were just so many pitches and every pitch had a list. You had to sign up and then fight to keep your place, but he said you could make a lot of money. He said there were violin players saving up to buy houses in the country. I knew that was bullshit.

Brixton. Charlie and his brother grew up in an orphanage in Brixton where his daddy who was a Cornish nationalist fascist had dumped them. Charlie said that busking in the London Underground was what had cured him of insanity – and that staying there would have driven him crazy all over again.

I met Charlie in Berlin, 1983.

You stood there holding the baby, I raged, I tore out the window frame/ **why are you doing this**/ I couldn't stop/ **my little brother and I**/ holding onto each other/ **wearing our plastic shoes**/ government issue/ **waving goodby**/ goodby daddy/ **see you next year**/ sniffing glue/ **why should I care**/ hut/ **two**/ three/ **four**/ SIG HEIL DADDY

I stood there holding the baby, you raged you tore out the window frame/ **why am I doing this**/ you couldn't stop/ **my little brother and I**/ marching in step/ **we couldn't stop**/ Daddy was calling us/ **we chanted kill the Pakkies**/ kill the Niggers/ our best friends were Pakkies and Niggers/ **but we tried TO HATE THEM FOR YOU**/ two/ **three**/ four/ **SIG HEIL DADDY**

You stood there holding the baby, I raged I tore out the window frame/ **why are you doing this**/ I couldn't stop/ **my little brother is marching in step**/
        my little brother is marching in step/
marching in step/
        marching in step/
                marching in step/
my little brother is marching in step/
        my little brother is marching in step/
every day/
        every day/
                every day/
                        every day

every day/
every day
OF HIS LIFE

Fred, I just had a really good shit/ **hast du cigaretten fur mich?**/
Friedrich, Friedrich, Friedrichstrasse, café, cigaretten, rum and vodka/
Friedrich, Friedrich, Friedrichstrasse, café, cigaretten, rum and vodka/
He denied me/ (picks up an empty tube of glue from the ground and sniffs)/ **just reminiscing**/ on New Year's Eve, the entire Berlin sky would light up with rockets – East and West united/fire in the sky. It was like the *Christopher Hour*, "And if everyone lit just one little candle, what a bright world this would be... " The punks in Kreuzberg scored some truly amazing rocket/candles and aimed them at bank windows. It looked like Beirut/**me neither**/ Charlie would have studied geography and Turkish drumming at the university of Kreuzberg, if there had been such a thing/ **but he was distracted from his studies by an all-consuming passion for**
marijuanna/**belladonna**/ heroin/**glue**
I just wanna make love to **you raged, you tore out the window frame**/ I stood there holding the/**you stood there holding the**/you stood there/**you stood**/you/
my little brother is marching in step/
my little brother is marching in step/
marching in step/
marching in step/
marching in step/

my little brother is marching in step/
> **my little brother is marching in step**/

every day/
> **every day**/
>> every day/
>>> **every day**
>> every day/
>>> **every day**

OF HIS LIFE

The beginning of the first week was party time, dope booze and steak…

The first time I met Charlie Savage he was asleep. I woke him up. It was 4:30 in the afternoon. We were on the top floor of an abandoned Nazi uniform factory that had been turned into an anarchist squat called the *Kukuck*. The beginning of the first week was party time. Dope booze and steak. By the third week of the month Charlie Savage was feeding the entire fourth floor of the Kuckuck – the Punks had spent their dole. Charlie was far from a big earner on the street, but he would not eat in front of hungry people/**MY LITTLE BROTHER IS MARCHING**/ in the orphanage in Brixton where they had a new art teacher who was young and idealistic. The art teacher loved the subject he was teaching and genuinely wanted to reach the boys. One day he brought his 8-year-old son to school to meet his students. His son was dressed neatly, but not expensively, and had brought his own art books to work in while his father taught the class. During the class, there was a phone call for the teacher. He left his son in the class while he answered the phone. The first thing Charlie and his friends did was to take the boy's books away from him and rip out the pages. By the time the father returned, they had dragged the boy – screaming – to the fountain outside the class and they were pushing him – headfirst – into the stagnant waters. Charlie couldn't stop himself. Charlie raged. By the time I met him, most of this rage was directed towards himself and window frames. Later on he got married, they had children and he even quit drinking, in Ireland of all places, by turning on to his own absolutely unique version of Jesus stood there holding the baby and said why are you doing this?

And Charlie couldn't answer.

Piccadilly Circus

It was just like a Paul Neuman movie, only I wasn't playing cool man Paul – I was playing the chump. We're in a stagecoach office, and the stage is just about to leave. Richard Boone walks in. He's the baddest ever Hollywood bad guy and he wants a ticket, but the coach is full. He looks around and sees Paul Neuman, who is playing a half-breed Indian (that's what they called him in the movie). The movie was called *Hombre*, and Paul was the hombre. So Richard Boone looks around, and being a bigoted asshole, he spies this "half-breed" Indian and says, "Right, I'll have his ticket."

Paul Neuman is cool. he doesn't say anything. He just sits there like he doesn't hear, but the chump –

that's me – says, "But that's not right. He was here first."

So Richard Boone says to the chump, "Right, I'll have your ticket."

So there I was finishing up my pitch at the bottom of the Piccadilly escalator. I was just about to stop playing. Little Stan the accordion man from Russia was there waiting for me to pack up, when one of the crackhead brothers from Birmingham shows up and says to me, "This is how saxophones get smashed up."

"What?"

"This is my pitch."

"No it's not. There's a list and you're not on it."

"You're stitchin' me up. I was here this morning and signed up for now."

"What time?"

"2:30."

"No, what time did you sign up?"

"11:00."

"I was here at 11:00. You weren't here."

"Maybe it was 11:30."

"Stan signed up at ten after."

"It's my pitch."

"Sorry, if you wanna play here, you have to come around in the morning and sign up."

"You gonna be sorry."

"Yeah?"

"You gonna be sorry."

"What are you gonna do, get your big brother?"

This stopped him for a minute. I'd been waiting for a chance to use this line ever since I'd heard Eric use it. The trouble is Eric was a big stroppy Scot who could pick a man up and pin him against the wall with one hand.

"You gonna be sorry," he said again. The crackhead brothers from Birmingham were not very bright, and I was talking to the stupid one.

I was kind of pissed off, because he'd threatened my saxophone. Also, I had low blood sugar because I was on a starvation diet at the time. This made me short tempered – it didn't do much for my intelligence either.

The crackhead brother from Birmingham shouldered Stan aside and set up his saxophone case by the escalator.

"But it's my pitch," said Stan, not sounding very much like Paul Neuman, but I was detinitely into playing the chump, because I picked up the crackhead's case and carried it over to the back wall. My stuff was all packed up by then, which was a good thing, because he threw it across the floor and charged me. I'm pretty much of a wimp, but he wasn't exactly Mike Tyson. He tried to butt me in the stomach, and I just grabbed him by the throat. I should have hung on and tried to fucking choke him to death. Instead, I held on, but only long enough to discourage him, then shoved him away and said, "I'm not gonna fight you."

There was no point, Stan the accordion man had pissed off.

"You fucked up my throat."

If I had any sense I would have ripped it out – but I didn't say that, I picked up my saxophone and said, "You better hope my saxophone's okay."

"You fucked up my throat."

"If you fucked up my saxophone, you're gonna be sorry."

"Yeah?"

"Yeah."

I was leaving by then and was just shooting off my mouth to save face. He followed me down the corridor away from the escalator.

"What are you gonna do?"

"You'll find out."

"What are you gonna do?"

"You'll see."

I was loaded down with all my gear, but his saxophone was out of sight by now, so I knew he wouldn't start anything.

"What are you gonna do?"

"You'll…."

I didn't know he was left-handed until his big hard left fist broke my nose. He followed it up with a pretty ineffectual attempt at head butting, but by then there was about a pint of my blood on the floor. We grappled for few minutes, I tried to push him down the stairs, but mostly I just bled on him until one of the staff came. The crackhead brother from Birmingham ran off, and I picked up my gear.

"You better leave the station," said the staff.

"I'm catchin' a train."

"You goin' home like that?"

"I got a ticket."

Poems by Gauranga Mohanta

A Maroon Blazer

A maroon blazer is flying. The chilliness of wind could not paint the blazer's wings with color of sluggishness. The warmth of a life is woven into the feathers. The blazer-feathers have got brilliance from the feel of youth arising out of the bonfire of the field, the savor of the pond surrounded by sal trees and the freeness of the border-house. Standing near the destination of the blazer is the nudity of the bench; here the feathers glow with happiness as they land. When the darkness falls on the bushes, the fruit flavour, prayer image are crafted on the tongue.

Phlox

The aroma of moonlight wafts down from all the lotus episodes. Anklets jingle a short distance away, in the faint sound the island evening attempts emit non-Aryan songs on the way home, insects tremble in the light of wild cotton plants, door opens before bird-waves reach a crescendo. Phlox spreads whiteness on the sofa and the velocious sky strives to seek colors of stars almost silently. The carpels of all plants of the world are sound-prone, a seeker's silence is not agreeable to a flower. Phlox teaches the sky how to pronounce interjections.

Beneath the Blue Ice

A terpsichorean's gesture became visible on the stage built on a skull as the globe deflated against the aridness of the forest; you have to stay in the dark tundra-house with a lifeless body. The buzz of microbes beneath the blue ice; the taste of intestine is of great importance to domesticated germs. Microbes are death-conscious, your tears have no implication to them. A morning feeds fire to make you desolate; in fire's fierceness the dry tree first discerns the path of Nirvana --the illusion of a purest face happens to be formless; gloomy dust does not fly around any road, your wailing is washed away by the sea water, screams seemingly choked off comes back over and over again.

Poems by Sarah Leavesley

at the end ~~of the year that shouldn't have happened~~

while re-reading MacNeice, endlessly

/ I don't cry // though I've tried to break the window that bays ~~hugs~~ back grief /// Pink roses tap against glass //// and snowflakes fall inside me ////

Without warm light to soften these crystals //// to sparkling, or water ///// there is no spilling ~~touch~~ / no gutter-surge or river pulse // no overflow suddenness ///

No pipped sorrow ~~kiss~~//// only hard ground //// that crackles more white noise //// than thawful glimmer-trap frost ///// beneath memory's crazy-glazed sunsteps /

I lasso the lost tears // as prayer beads /// mind-stroke the stone days //// that fidget in my frozen fingers //// Chipped fragments ~~miss~~ precipitate ////

bone splinters ///// I don't cry though /

Your Survival Bunker

i)

You don't remember how you got here. Only that you wake to find yourself alone, scrunched up in a tight ball. Strangely, there's comfort in the lack of light, a sense of space folding in around you, almost as tight as a blanket, if not as warm as a hug.

Luckily, ghosts don't eat much, and you can't imagine ever feeling hungry again, so you've no need for heavy cans or tin-openers, only memories and emotions. You have plenty of these.

For at least a few months after your apocalypse, pain seeps from every pore. You're sure you're on own forever, though reason tries to argue that this isn't true but those still living can smell your wounded heart and are avoiding you like the plague.

The ones that do try to contact you, send messages which you ignore. Denial is your only lifeline. Meanwhile, phantoms rush once more to feast on you, though no one knows to help because these teeth don't leave tangible bite marks.

By the time it's finally safe to come out, the salt from your tears could preserve your whole body.

ii)

When you emerge post-everything, that first air tastes sweeter than condensed milk sucked though a small hole in a tin, though it still feels difficult to swallow.

You may notice your fingers tapping a strange rhythm against hard surfaces like the remnants of a desperate Morse code. Register this, but don't allow yourself surprise until you start to keep pace with background music, or hum along to new tunes.

Putting your hand in your pocket now, you find a hanky that's still dry.

International Swimming Pool Rules

1. No ducking, bombing or diving, unless on command from the Pentagon.

2. Lifeguards are there to guard. Please obey their orders respectfully and promptly. The guns are (mostly) only there for show.

3. Maximum capacity – has already been reached. Crisis lines and camps are in the process of being set up. Please wait elsewhere until they're open.

4. No flippers, buoyancy aids or inflatables. These are to be kept for when sea levels rise another ten feet.

5. Evacuation procedure. Please swim carefully to the nearest exit. Middle-aged white men with Armani suits and bank balances over a billion dollars will be given priority. Everyone else should prepare to sink or swim, swim or sink.

6. Do not panic if your eyes start to sting and you feel strong chemicals fill your lungs. These are essential for effective cleansing.

7. No screaming.

Poems by Bimal Guha

The Swan

If the silver rain comes down and measures my existence with a deep kiss, I will also say with a grin, o nature, open the outer door. I will also harmonize with the river voice to be merged with the ocean tides. I will put my hands on a woman's chest and spread rain onto her eyes resembling those of a speechless statue and touch her body to develop a close intimacy; like roaring floodwater I will swallow two steep banks.

If the swollen river flows through countryside and swallows troubled areas while running through the valley, the kids wake up--running in houses with joy, rejoicing at the joy of water. Rows and rows of swans glide on the cradle of waves. I raise my hands to give them a clap.

Rub-a-dub

Rub-a-dub, rub-a-dub, the chest trembles in an instant; the terrestrial sphere trembles; the inward spirit and human sensibilities tremble. All the time, rub-a-dub reverberates in the chest in my sleep stages and waking states. Is Ukraine a victim of tigers--body wounded by claws? Is Russia a naked paw or a bomb that shakes atmosphere? Is the earth an enigma of unballanced globe, a coil of smoke--toxic carbon ashes? Does the human conscience which is also bereft of humanity bear a resemblance to the molten iron or an arid desert without trees? Rub-a-dub reverberates in the chest. A poisonous stream of boiling lava flows into the warm nostrils. Rub-a-dub, Rub-a-dub, the inward spirit trembles and trembles all the time. Rub-a-dub, rub-a-dub, the crippled beats make the terrestrial sphere shudder.

A Full Moon in the Sky

I reached your house in sweltering noonday heat. You looked preoccupied with thoughts as you stretched your shapely legs on the sofa! A beam of sunlight clung to your body like a greedy libertine. I spotted the difference between you and the sun from a distance. Two lotus-bumblebees were playing on your feet. You were perfectly in tune with the view. Were you scared to see my standing shadow? When the bees of your desire hailed me waving their hands, the sun went down. Then ten tame bees were flying and playing in the shadow of my body. The evening approached. Your face turned out gloomy as soon as I unfurled my wings like a bird that would be back to its nest. Urged to extravagances I touched you at one time. And the shimmering moonlight reached out to the door. In the half-light and semi-darkness you emerged as stunningly beautiful. As the night wore on I spread some moonlight on your body and face. Then there was a full moon in the sky. Like a winter's night, fog rolled in from your eyes.

All of them translated from Bangla by Gauranga Mohanta

Poems by Brontë Elizabeth Page

Art

All my life I have been lied to, for all my life I have been taught, that Galleries were a guise to view the greatest art in the world. Now I lie too, as what I write will never be as beautiful as you: but this statement is simply not true, and my great art must be foretold to you.

The greatest art I have ever witnessed is you and I, living under the same sky. That night we spent, our bodies intertwined, our souls twined like vines through our hearts, a compass to our bodies, and the stars are guide, as we grow with passion and lustful whines. With the stars, how they shine, they were our guide, giving us light in a once nefarious night, like you, they gave light in the darkest time.

You and I, I'm sure we were a heavenly sight; for we felt the greatness of this night, this beautiful moment, with all our might. This was art of our own creation, and it was but met with our own admiration. We are not framed on a Gallery wall, deemed greatness for all, it was just for us: this anthropological art.

You and I, under the same sky, art needs no explanation, so I will not ask "Why?", but my eyes do nearly cry, knowing that you love I, and we experienced a beauty under the sky, a moment I will cherish to the day I die. In moments of beauty, magic becomes true, and there is no better grandeur than myself under you.

That night was beautiful. That night was yearning, (occurring), Olympic ululation: you and I, in utter elation. We were not witnessed by a Galley or viewers, as then touch will become tyrannous, but that was not our art, our love was pure and will be evermore. We are the only people are art was for the stars and us, as I become ichor with though of this night, as love becomes life, that is blithe.

The stars watched, and smile as they knew, that I have always been yours, and you have been mine too. The stars and the moon know how special we are, and how greatness for two did not travel far yet there was a time I did not know who you are and thoughts of love, I did mar. But here you are, under the stars, making the artist a work of art. Painting my life with love and lust. I know this beauty, unlike us, will never thrust.

The stars watched, as you became mine, as we became constellations in nefarious night, shinning bright, a beacon of light. Hope for the past when love was just might, yet now we know those stories were right. Now you and I, bodily we pry, you painted my life with nothing but delight, vividly with viridity, as I now try to write of the beautiful art we made that night

You and I, and the stars all witnessed art, the greatest art, the universe of stars knows this is true and that art was fated for two: you and I when our bodies elated. Stars shine in the dark, as like us, they have witnessed true beauty in art, 'tis this that lets them shine in the dark, of when our love was so stark.

This was truly the greatest art there is no Gallery, but it will always be a beautiful memory in my own collection, a painting that is so often in my recollection. We won't be framed in a gallery wall, but framed in my heart, his sculpture so divine that is entirely mine. An ethereal night, transcendent is right, as I try to write the beautiful art we created that night.

Macabre Is Life Death Is Nice

When your light goes out, and the world goes black, you know you lose your chance of ever coming back; and realise that living can be just as dead as dead, till the sight of her black you no longer dread.
As everyone I see is filled with joy and ecstasy and in the middle, there is me dreaming of joy that will never beas I am me and always this will be. The world has not been comfort to me so I just dream of joy and of the boy dreaming of love that will never be. Goodbye to ecstasy as it will never be. I dream of Death taking my final breath leaving life is no misery to me perhaps in death joy and ecstasy will enrobe me. Let us wait and see, till we no longer see.

Rain Won't Make The Blossom Grow It Will Drown Them.

Spring has sprung, Spring has sprung, but in it the depths of misery hath begun. In fields of blossom, I see but one. A bittersweet taste, as my last Spring I face, till my time on Earth is done. Spring has sprung, Spring has sprung. In fields of blooming death will run, yet mourning hath not begun. For why morn a rose, that blooms with Spring blossom, singing for hours- but there is nothing but superfluity it is bringing. Now with scrupulous Spring's sprung, my death hath begun. Spring has sprung, Spring has sprung. With Springs sprung, death hath begun and I realise now, that I was always a flower for you to deflower; one by one, now like the three months of Spring, I am done. Spring has sprung- Death has sprung, Death has sprung.

Poems by Laura Whelton

Blueberry Kisses

You stretched the warmth of my skin bear with delicate, soft, golden touches, whilst I bathe in vanilla milk waters, deep, this flows like Autumnal rains lightly brushing silken, moonbeamed gossamer threads laid out willingly to bask in your aura, a glint of light varnishes the cracks of me, this tangible thought embedded on a single second-breaks, as dawn sings in the sky the clouds have lifted.

Dub No Bass with My Head Man (Underworld song title)

Bitter pills, swallowed regrets- truth, a fragrant assailant thoughts churning, vomiting in magnitude banging diseased equilibrium, devoted to your sensory Gods- all over nothing; senseless lies, games playing hiding dervishes, whirling motion, tornados of avarice caught in the eye of the storm, vacant emptiness propositioned-hellish slander of a once cherished friend sunk again into depths of hatred careless abandonment- wrecked demons of this- what we thought we knew continuously.

Dreamscape 1

Flying through houses shadows of people, insipid ; A building unknown. Three cars lost and can't find the keys; someone is in a house I can't get to suspension, fear; you drive me into the shallow water. My legs are torn but we laugh and run with a stranger; dark, library guy locking gates at sunset. The light illuminates the river and the old grey car still against. The bed of eels glistening, now a boat; the sun falls on this mirage of beautiful pain- flying, running, awake.

Poems by Obayed Akash

Impulses

The football always pursues him instantly. In allusion! Into the intense amicability! The midday fervidness of the dense forest makes him febrile. He, the health-conscious football-feverish rookie, has been tending for the fruitless luxury. He has assumed that the minimal fire vertex in the burning chimney is the prime source of illumination. Any type of power source makes him fascinated: for instance - Football. Football is forever the restless origin of dynamics. The world - we may convince the world as a delusive metaphor, and certainly, it's a planet of definite velocity. Otherwise, cosmic images could decipher that the world is nothing but an extraordinary football. Whatever it is, things that are falling apart or flying over: such as crops, golden bugs -, explains about the centrepiece of creation is football. Whether streaming or swimming in the sea or in a ditch, whatever it is - but who knows on which way, that very emotion-feverished man should have flown away!

Poet Abdul Hassan had no regret for the rusty keys of the UN

Am I alright, am I really fine? All through the days and nights, laying on a privy entity, you're suffering the careless disease, yet portraying yourself so self-confident. King comes and king goes, now the flood has submerged the long been unprotected vast paddy fields around. You, the very seizer, clutched him by his hair and thrown him into a rotten muddy pond, and with calm sighing, you thought that - now your polite sister could accomplish in red shari without trouble. But if you pursued her obvious cause: you had remained melancholy to you own solicits. Again, in a while, if all this undeniably loveliness becomes suitable for you- the UN could never be reconciled. Since that you've been thinking, touches of melancholy have no vernacularly. The magic stone that possesses the grace, you have tried to decipher its inner worth, you sacrificed your life Abul Hassan, became no more in this world. As far your father was alive, he had been a man of little worth, holding fragrant flowers in his hand. Till you couldn't reconcile if you had seen burying a female cadaver. Till death, you had an appropriate sense of the disparity between a man and a policeman. In this sadden country of arisen, betel-leaves turn green to yellow, reminding us that we had forgotten the charity of the nature. Still, we like to pretend, we are doing fine probably (?), so, how are you doing Abul Hassan!

Metropolis

Very recently my Metropolis-affinity has increased beyond horizons. Once, I mistaken the pungent smell of burnt-petroleum and delusively proclaimed it as glimmering grasses; my well-wishers clanged me and then admitted to lunatic asylum- where at there I outcry vehemently: "mother! mother!! watch, how efficiently your son is metamorphosing to a metropolitan boy!". I water the metropolis every morning, assuming it's the inheritor of our porch-garden floras back home. And at deep late-night sleep, play with shepherd boys, we mimicry- one of our brown calf or black goat has get lost each twilight. At this Metropolis on air, radio or laying on park bench listen folks, spiritual, lyrical music, keep watching…, the crying newlywed girl going for new home leaving behind the native home or married woman happily coming back to visit parents by boat roaming through the overflowing river, or the broken-lover singing sad-ballads on his unspecified journey. Soon I'll arrange a ritual invitation, offer traditional treats and sweetmeats and then I'll explain to them what's going on with my recently acquired Metropolis-affinities.

All of them were translated by Ashoke Kar

Poems by Pijush Kanti Barua

Mate of Thoughts

My village is just at a kissing distance to river Karnaphuli. Her amity revives the village in summer and winter but causes dying danger during the monsoon. Engine boats make transportation easier but cause erosion to the banks. Father's huge betel-nut orchard, uncle's home-ground, to the north someone else's graves and tombs, all are now underwater. The river is a bank less wonder to me since my childhood. Voyage on her surface by Sampan towards the city and the festive sight of the Kalurghat red bridge was the endless waves of imagination to me regarding the river. The river is a boat of thoughts in my every breathing, as it were, carrying a bunch of fables floating from the hills far away. The river is my soulmate. The waste products of paper-mills, cadavers of cows, sacrificing Durga-idol, releasing Manosha idol or the sorrows of moving tribes and sometimes flock of water-plants, for all such things, river is the splendid shelter. The power of maintaining equality by the river is infinite and her affection is brimless too. River is the flame-wick of the fishermen-life. River is the bridge of communication between inhabitants of both banks. She is the listener to the melancholy songs of the village-bride who awaits for her elder brother to take her back to visit paternal home. It is the source of proteins for the fish-prone population. River means floating men sailing towards traceless destination by bamboo-raft. River is my vehicle of happiness with full of creativity. In the stairs of life, river bears immortal streams, tales of water and whispers of sands. River brings memories to anxious ears, brings smell of sun, unveils the science of hunting of white cranes, exhibits the juggling of banana-bearing boats and radiates the wisdom of oars of tired boatman. River of my childhood is my luxury of dreaming in my deep meditating sleep. Today, thousands of years have been passed walking through life with clouds trailing the turns at Ajanta in bashfulness. Childhood days reach the sky today and the sky touches the earth of life. Melodies of river become feeble reaching streets of cities which are chariots of dreams to achieve goals. Juggler time metaphors the sun into an omelette. Noon-ending festival awakes in the cafe of time and among all these combinations, my thought-mate, the Karnaphuli, seems to be a miracle golden island of beyond earthly boons in the Milky Way.

Walking

One, who walks, knows the challenges of walking. How deep are the feelings of a pedestrian of thousand years, knew Jibanananda after walking to Cinamon Island. Journey by walking shows the world dividing and indicates how the world map and the continents became loose moving apart from each other. Walking enables to understand what the distances are made between fingers and palms. A pedestrian knows what else lose contacts due to walking. Walking discriminates between white and black, East and West, believers and atheists. It separates father from son, homestead from dweller, rituals from laws. Walking differentiates among Ram-Rahim-Ananda-Anthony. Walking shows clouds taking the forms of different female faces and colours of the gesturing sky of Elora. Walking brings enliven cave-arts of Ajanta in front, migratory clouds team with dust of time. Walking brings oneself to the last end of a populating land, disappears the tired pedestrian to the horizon, walking stops life in a dark cage. A pedestrian knows well what his losses are walking life-long.

Inevitable Fear

It's incredible to survive so many years facing the attempts to be destroyed one after one; sometimes, from Bigbang to pulverized constellation or on the lifeboat during Noah's arc. Sometimes in the distorted Hiroshima due to the devastating atomic cyclone of the Second World War, it was attempted to kill me, but still, I'm alive with infinite boons of time. I were to die in Crusade, I were to die in Kurukshetra, my breath was entrapped in the battlefield of Kalinga. But even then, my beating heart didn't stop. No landslide could abolish me nor could any tsunami-tide. I returned from Haiti and Nepal with my life. But still, I triumph with my endangered life. Everywhere I found rows of dead bodies of hope surrounding me. Dreams are killed and the bloodstream runs to all directions. Today I, who survived all attempts of being killed, am at risk. I feel death is confirmed in the era of rotten youth.

Poems by Ashoke Kar

At the last scene I realized: I'm dead!

Scene One:

Everything has changed, everything, life seems a replica painting on the wall or an old, discoloured snapshot in the album, radiating spirits of life to a desperate man, who wants to respirate! I woke up in the middle of a day, and sleepwalked all through the night; did I really sleep at night? That's a mystery! I do go back to my past, walk into my memories-, I could see my future even, and then unconsciously try to resolve my zig-saw puzzles piece by piece. Only at the present, I can't roam around; in the mirror, my reflexions are unnatural, like surreal images. I feel myself a different self, a person who is trying to recreate my past and future to scroll the present. Often, I refuse, pretending that I'm not that guy probably, who is reflecting myself in the mirror!

Last night I woke up from sleepwalking; into the mist of warm vapour of my bathtub, I could listen and count my breathing, as I can hear the footsteps coming toward or going away from me. Even with all my surprise, I can hear the footsteps of my immediate past and of my near future! That's the way I decide my destinations in my sleepwalk. So last night I decided to revisit what I did with three roses, those I picked up from the neighbouring flower shop. The young man at the flower shop is a poet, who keeps 3 fresh and pretty roses daily for me. He said I didn't show up for almost a week. I was confused, I think he has mistaken as poets are forgetful or he was not at the shop while I was there. But I never argue. He is a nice guy, he likes me and technically, he is a poet. I like his choices of matching roses, he does it for me always. To make him happy, I said, I'm broke, so I had broken the rule. He smiled, then murmured:

Sometimes breaking the rules is just
extending the rules
Sometimes there are no rule …

Scene Two:
Wow, beautiful! Every word seems written only for me. How does he know, how I going through recently; nothing is normal-, and nothing is abnormal either. I'm making and breaking rules. But I'm not going to tell that to anyone, rather I patted his shoulder again, told him, wow, nice poem, you did great! He handed me over the bouquet of flowers, a triangle of pink, yellow and white roses with somber smell. Then whispered, "It's not me, I just recited Mary Oliver's poem!" I patted on his shoulder again, 'One day, it would be you!' With my insight I visualized, the middle-aged him, standing by the podium and applause ringing all through the dim light of the ballroom; audiences are on their feet, honouring him a standing ovation. Suddenly, I started feeling lonely, I thought I'm late. Someone in somewhere has been waiting for my roses! That's why I buy roses for her every day. But at this moment, memory

betrayed me, I'm unable to recollect, who she was..., and where should I go!

Scene Three:

To hide my embarrassment, I stepped forward. I forgot to greet '...bye' to the poet. Instead, with every step, I tried to visualize a face, to whom I'm carrying these roses; to whom my heart is belonged to..., how far should I go! I passed the monument on the crossing, and all of a sudden, I discovered Munses' 'Cry' has been radiating panic from the wall graffiti. Panicked I'm, swiftly tried to pass away the graffiti and probably I stepped over the old lady, who were feeding folks of pigeons. Pigeons just flew away as I approached very near to them absentmindedly. Still, I'm hearing their flapping wings surrounding me. Still, I'm feeling the wind of their flapping wings, it reminded me that, I don't have my wings, but my mind is flying. I reached the arched bridge, stood by the railing, watching the water beneath the arch. I found myself. My image is on the water surface. This is the third time I'm here, watching my image, onto the same spot, same water, with three roses holding in hand, and I did let them go away. Because I can't remember anymore to whom these roses are belonged to. So l let the bouquet of flowers go away. It quietly sliced the thin air, dropped and broke my image into pieces. Pieces of my image scattered around the water and I lost myself again.

Surprisingly, there has no last scene...

Poems by Thida Mommaitri

Loss

I remember the way you ran your fingers across my face ever so gently, your soft gaze peering down at me. touching my lips softly with your fingertips, blue eyes, freckles like stars across your nose radiating your warmth onto my skin. but our passion ignited flames and all I have left of you are the ashes from the home we built.
-yours truly,
thida

Culture

I am from the sound of ramen bubbling in the pot, the smell of fresh Thai food wafting into my room, boba drinks on the run to the Asian market. golden temples shining in the vibrant sunlight and walking down the pier to the floating market to see the array of street foods available. I'm proud to be Thai
-yours truly,
thida

Growth

She wears her heart on her sleeve so fearlessly. still
believing that she is worthy of love, even though time
after time people have convinced her she was nothing
but a body, a mother's inconsistent toxic love an
absentee and abusive father but she grew to recognize
her toxic patterns from the way she grew up, she is
growing, healing, evolving. loving herself when she
feels like she can't loving every part of herself she used
to hate. she is me and I am her.
-yours truly,
thida

Poems by Tajalla Sattar

Damnation

Her words lose control whenever she holds her pen and rage like some wild ocean, she holds within herself a tsunami of emotions. Her voice trembles and her hands quiver, still she roars her truth using some ink and paper. They call her a black sheep, an abomination like she really asked for their validation. She's an erupted volcano, a fierce being who writes her own tale, her own destiny. She watches the world falling into the pits of darkness, sins becoming the new ordinary. Day after day the news of despair and grief gives her a purpose to use her imagination. Her words simply try to protect the world from eternal damnation.

A Valley of Secrets

Quite often she sits alone with her mind in reverie and even though her heartfelt sorrow pierces though her words and the darkness of her soul can be seen through her eyes, she refuses to settle for anything less than she desires. And just like a pitch-black winter night, she gives shivers down their spine, like some holily spirit walks by her side to hold her hand and lit her way through the eeriest paths of that deadly valley where the secrets of her heart reside.

Walking Dead

I see hollow bodies walking down the streets, empty hearted, soulless but faking their smiles to make sure no one notices the pain they go through. I hear the anguish screams of the voiceless
who suffer but can't make a move. Of those who feel safe in the grasp of their own arms because this world is not really a place for such kind hearts. I witness people pulling the strings of their fate, trying to mend their broken parts but with every new blow they fall apart. No matter how hard they try to hide in their shells just to find a moment of solace. To breathe a sigh of relief before going back to the same old path. It feels like a marathon, a struggle to keep going when all they want is to end this agony. Sometimes it feels like a never-ending cycle, their only fate when they're left with no choice but to simply stay. In a daily grind of life and in all this worldly mess all they wish for is just a fresh new start.

Poems by Lipi Nasrin

The aroma of loneliness

Now-a-days I nourish the emptiness in me. I used to manage kindling fire causing friction between pieces of stone. Some obscure faces resembling rhizome lie down beneath the surface. Sometimes your ariel branch comes down, sometimes you dive into an abyss. I search the aroma of shrivelled rose-petals preserved in my book. The blue clouds of the autumn kiss the catkin flowers. You have been diversified knowing my love. An unseen bumblebee comes to me again and again. My dismal love-cocoon awaits silky end. I terribly suffer the sharp pang of loneliness. Suddenly I draw an image with the colour of chickpea. I see the tailorbird seeking the refuge in the green leaf blade. Happy end of my waiting is adorable, but yearning is the sweetest one. I sweeten the aroma of yearning into my chest and shoulder.

The silhouette

The evening fell from the eucalyptus into the chest of vegetable hummingbird. The dim ray of crepuscular merges into the era. Someone's picture, I am obsessed with, becomes lucid piercing the reddish horizon. Who are you? Flustered, I am in the grip of incurable obsession. The failing sight of my eyeball makes me tired not seeing you. The darkness descends in the forest, the fickle lyrics untie tinkling anklets to escape the sight of reality. The stars are flooded by the scented breeze, I keep on waiting to be dazzled. I glean the colours of light for the umpteenth time. But who are you? Unknown chum from far era, I spread out my canopy of love for you. With deep affection, I am finding out the silhouette unmindfully at late hour.

The old desire

The sky has aroused the old desire in me. Maybe it'll come running, invisible, a strange wave of mirage touches my feelings. The trees, parallel to roads, stroll with the small water bodies; large void fields gradually becoming insipid, but the wind blows and bends for making some obeisance to the nature. In early days, I was befriended by the wind which hid its face into my hair coloured with henna. That wind is no more, those trees are more matured, and the water of the reservoir has evaporated aspiring to be fulfilled by the rain. Now they make a face at me, I am unwanted to their uncanny lyrics. The sky spanning the horizon is not mine, the floating blue clouds remain obscure to me. My vision swims in disappeared city. Our evanescent odor exists in the white petals of Nyctanthes.

Poems by Dayal Dutta

Acting!

There is no end to the story! Where someone's story stops Someone else's story begins. The stories are like stories. Some stories are true, some are fantasies! The stories wet with tears my dearest; I enjoy the beauty of life in intense pain. To tell a happy story, to listen Who doesn't want? There is a kind of joy hidden in howling loudly, the pain of the mind is alleviated, albeit a little; who can dare to share the stories of suffering? You want to hear the story all night, the story of life! I, you, we are the story Analogy. Sometimes you act never or I.

Release

The cosmopolitan monster has returned in form, sectarianism in countries, communalism in people! Science believers are humiliated on the pretext of religion, a village after village is burning with the violence of fundamentalists. Peaceful society in the grip of aggression. Sustainable development in the wake of climate change, building society is on the rise; the disruptive environment is extended. Inadequate food supply, famine in public life. In nuclear toxic emissions, the system is progressively wound. People want to be released!

New oath

The foundation of the industry is for those who touch with Love. In the labour of day labourers. The vastness of the earth, and the smell of workers' sweat all over the walls of the empire. The stories of suffering are horrible, tortured screams and big helpless! The farmer who spends all his labour on grain production to starving children in his house, building construction workers are homeless, equitable distribution of resources. The affluence of the aristocracy. Irregularities, irregularities and corruption now enslave the lords. By wanting a more desolate nature, subculture, anti-politics-- ordinary people who are oppressed. Socialism is very much needed in today's society, Ordinary people want love, want food and shelter; family members want to breathe a sigh of relief. Although it is too late, the time has come today, to take a new oath to Be one of the workers of the world.

Part Four

Short Stories

Swakrito Noman

Yudhishthira's Dog

Yudhishthira said, this dog is my disciple, I wish to take it with me. Indra said, one who belongs to a dog can't be allowed to enter into the heaven. Yudhishthira said, I can't disavowal a dog for my own ease.
-Mahabharata. Mahasthanikparva

Getting down to the corner of the Farmhouse if one start walking along Indira Road towards Farmgate, a raw market can be seen. Right in the middle of the market under the short banyan tree of footpath on the road near the dustbin of City Corporation, a flabby dog can be seen lying down. Such a flabby dog is rare to be seen in the town. Its body may become such flabby after having leftovers of the dustbin. or it is lazy. It doesn't take an effort to hanker after food whole day. Or it may happen, any incurable disease has taken root in its body. Otherwise, it wouldn't be like this type of awkward. Who becomes so flabby just because of eating? Other dogs of this market, do they eat less? They are not as flabbier as it.

It sleeps whole the day right next to the dustbin. It may sleep. Or it gets relaxed closing its eyes. It may lose energy to stand so lay down the whole day by pressing its head to the chest like that. It doesn't' move even if mosquito fly sits on it, It doesn't startle with the sharp horn of the car, too. Maybe it has become used to live with citizen noise. Sometimes if there is any scrimmage with left over of dustbin it sees at a glance by raising its head, after that it nods its head near to its chest as usual. Thinks, what else is this. This kind of scrimmage happens often. Other dogs of the market don't come very close to the edge of it. They don't mix with it. They even don't dare to disturb it. Sometimes they come to sniff its body. They try to understand whether it is alive or dead. They stand for a little while, move the tail, make hi, itch body, then leave slowly.

Nobody sees when the dog eats. Whether the dog eats anything or not within the whole day nobody knows. As it is not a person. Nobody has any headache even whether the people in park and footpath are having anything or starving. It is a hollow dog, is there anybody who will keep an eye on its having food or starving. Maybe it eats. The leftover of the Sunmoon restaurant situated on the other side of the market that gathers on the dustbin at night, in the last portion of the night, when the other dogs kept sleeping, then it gets up slowly and eats with full stomach. It doesn't eat anything whole day. It doesn't need to eat. Even some nights it spends without eating. Specially on rainy nights it doesn't eat anything. Under the bench of evicted passenger camp, it does have a profound sleep whole night. When the rain stops it comes to the previous place and lays down. Lying in one position one day passed.

Nobody notices that a dog is lying in one place day after day. Maybe somebody notices. But nobody has any headache of it. Is it any matter of headache? How much work people do, how busy people are? Day and night people are running......running. Where is the time for people to shake heads of good and bad of a dog?

One person thinks---kashiram cobbler, sitting on one side beside the footpath under the banyan tree. While cleaning boxes looking at the dog he asks it every morning, what's up flabby dog? How are you? The dog moves its ears then. Pulling its head it barks once. that's how it responses. Then it places to lay its head in again. If anyone removes the foam from the mouth calling flabby flabby whole day, it will not raise its head. It became habituate hearing those two words for a long day. Hearing those words, it can identify whose voice is this. It becomes its duty to respond then. And Kashiram has become habituated to utter these two words every day. If one day he misses to utter those he feels that the day will not go well, there will be no customer, he will be beaten by the police.

Most of the time of the day Kashiram's eyes remain fixed on the dog. The busiest area of the town is Indira Road. The customer comes frequently, no leisure time to scratch the nose even. Most of them are boot shoes. Sandals rarely come. If comes, comes only to polish. He doesn't have to sew. Dhaka is the city of rich men, who come with torn shoes? While brushing shoes the hands and the head of Kashiram moves with equal rhythm, and the eyes remain fixed on the dog. Kashiram has become habituated to staring at the dog while brushing. His eyes went to that side unknowingly. Even if the eyes turn to the other side within a moment, it gets fixed in the previous place again. Staring at it he recalls that Yudhishthira's dog often. In his childhood he heard about Yudhishthira's dog from his master. He can still remember it clearly.

While Kashiram starts to pack his boxes to come back home at night, he looks at the dog for the last time. Then he wishes to ask, what's up flabby, won't eat? Sometimes he asks. The dog then doesn't respond. Why doesn't it respond? Maybe it can't accept Kashiram's leaving. That is why it huffs.

Actually, Kashiram feels one kind of affection for this dog. It is natural to grow affection for it. How many days he knows it for! How many days they are together for! Aren't they together! What is the difference between the footpath of the banyan tree and the dustbin! Before three years while he was sitting under the banyan tree with his boxes from then he is seeing this dog. Then the age of the dog was less. Its health was not like this. Its body was oily and tight. It showed its power over all the market. No other dog could ever be successful in snatching the food. It was searching for food all the time. It sticked out its tongue all the time. It has no choice of food. Whatever eatable it gets in front, it would take it in its mouth. And now and then standing beside the wall of the dustbin it empties its bladder pulling it's one leg. Sometimes it evacuated even. Then Kashiram used to be very angry. Then he recalled that speech heard from the mouth of his headmaster in childhood: the person who has a dog, will not be allowed to enter heaven. His eyes and nose got frowned in hatred then. He threw old sandals shoes, whatever he got to the dog. Damn it, bastard! Didn't you get any place to evacuate! One day he threw a whole stammer towards its head. The dog ran to the opposite side of the road snorting. It didn't fall under the wheel of the bus for a little while. It would be flattened within a moment if there wouldn't a speed breaker. After that, the dog was not seen for so many days. Kashiram thought that it got dead or what! Maybe not. The life of a dog, would it die so easily? Maybe it left the area being scared. Or it is in the market still, it is not coming around Kashiram by being scared.

After some days Kashiram saw while he was coming back after having breakfast from Sunmoon restaurant, two dogs are penetrating on the footpath of the other side of the road. They are panting by keeping their tongue out. There lies a trace of fear in their eyes. Kashiram noticed that between them, there is that dog, to which head he threw the stammer. He rolled his eyes fast. He looked around whether anyone was seeing him or not. What a matter of shame. Though it was between the dogs, as it is a matter which happens between human being likely. If people found him staring at such a naked scene, what would they think about him? Bringing a line of laughter in his face he sat down on his place fast. But is peeling one's eyes always easy if you want? People of the road are staring wide eyed on that scene. A gentleman wearing pants-suit and tie was walking staring at that and seemed to push and fall with the nut seller. He didn't fall for a while. Moreover, the school was over. Students are coming back home. The scenery can't be avoided even from their eyes. The tiny conductor of leguna is making fun of it by making sound.

Kashiram anger then rises in the head. Damn, the dog of bitch! Isn't there any place to penetrate! From the back side a vegetable vendor complained against the City Corporation by asking what's going on? Why don't they arrange to kill the dogs? Hearing that the anger of Kashiram raised higher. Picking up a piece of bamboo he crossed the road without any pause and hit the dog hard on its head. But the injury didn't hit the head, it hit on the spot, along the middle of the two hips. The joint spot that had been clinging for a long time separated with one blow. After getting released the two sexually exhausted animals ran away towards two different ways.

About a year after taking the dog's seat near the dustbin. At that time target killing was going on all over the country. If today here so tomorrow there. The North-South-East-West are being stained with blood. Writer, publisher, teacher, Islamic religious leader, foreigner, priest, preacher are being sacrificed by chapati. The killer is throwing people in public, nobody is coming forward to save the attacked people. Who wants to be sacrificed by chapati? Who wants to be a target of the killers? They are making corpses in front of the police, the attack is on the police themselves, and their public is public.

On that morning the dog was in front of the Sunmoon restaurant. There were crowds of people inside the restaurant. The messiah couldn't be capable enough of supplying breakfast. It's 8.00 am in the morning. It's getting to be office time. Everyone is busy. The customers are chasing messier for breakfast again and again. The dog was chewing the nehari[1] sitting under the gas oven. As a customer hurried while entering into the restaurant, his eyes went there. With congested nose and face he said the soliloquy, disgusting environment. The ears of manager couldn't ignore it. Seeing the dog his anger also raised. Getting up from the chair, he took the long sticky fry pan of singara[2] and chased the dog. Leaving that bone the dog came running up the street. Then the person who sells chitoi[3] cake, he took a burning stick from the oven and threw it at it. It was missed. Won't it be? Dogs are careful animals. Seeing the rising hand of the cake seller up, it sensed the danger. After getting the signal, it ran away. The stick fell at the feet of a pedestrian.

On the other hand, there was a commotion. A man is running towards Farmgate from farmhouse junction. He is wearing pants, white vest on his body and leather sandals on the feet. Two young men are chasing him. Chap-dari[4] on one's face, wearing pajama panjabi. And the other one is a clean shaved face, wearing pants shirt. Both of them were carrying two black bags on their back and they were having sharp chapati in their hands. Kashiram was cleaning his boxes. His chest throbbed seeing the chapati shining in the light of the young sun. A few days ago, one of the priests was strangled to death in Pabna. A threat has been sent to the hierarch of Ramakrishna Mission. Leaving the boxes, he also ran away. The pedestrians are running wherever they can. On duty constable of the turn of the road entered the restaurant. Vegetable vendors, chicken sellers, the grocers, betel leaf sellers, cigarette sellers, cake sellers, nut sellers, mixed savoury snack sellers are fleeing.

When the man came running in front of the dustbin, one of the two chapati holders from behind stroke on his neck. Stroke felt on his back instead of his neck. Then the dog was under the bench of the passenger camp. Suddenly, barking loudly, it rushed to the spot with lightning speed. Seeing it coming forcibly one of the chapati holders started running towards the other side of the road. Until then aiming at the victim's neck another person stroked the second blow. The torso and head would be separated, if not, the dog would have bitten the chapati holder's leg. The victim fell face down on the road. His white vest began to get wet with blood. The killer stroke the chapati to the back of the dog to get rid of it. But the stroke fell to the ground. Slipping his feet, he fell upside down. The chapati fell from his hand. Then the dog climbed on his chest and bit his chin. Removing the dog from the chest in one fell swoop the killer sat up fast. This time the dog bit his leg. The killer stood with his arms folded. Then he ran away. The dog ran after him, barking at the sound of its throat cracking.

The dog stopped near the Farmgate over bridge. It looked for the killer. It didn't get. On that side there is huge number of people. The killer mixes with the crowd of people. The dog ran and came back to the victim again. The man is still lying face down. Didn't die. The fleeing pedestrians stopped this time. They keep coming towards the spot. Kashiram also comes out from behind the banyan tree. Vegetable vendors, chicken sellers, grocers, betel leaf sellers, cigarette sellers, cake sellers, nut sellers and mixed savoury snack[5] sellers kept coming forward.

In a short while, a crowd of people gathered around the injured man. A pedestrian pulls a mobile phone from his pocket and immediately took a picture of the victim. Even the constable came out of the restaurant quickly. Who knows if it sees his new clothes or cane in his hand or not, the dog started barking? The constable raised his cane and threatened it. Then the dog started barking louder.

The crowd of people continues to grow gradually. The dog then stood close to the wall of the dustbin, back to the east, it started urinating towards the crowd with its left leg raised. It got the emergence of urination. With a scatter-brained it began to empty its bladder.

Translated by Sayma Monica

Inoculation of translator:

1. Nehari: Nehari is the stew from the Indian sub-continent consisting of slow cooked meat, mainly shank meat of beef or goat along with bone marrow.

2. Singara: Singara is one kind of cake can be taken as snacks.

3. Chitoi: Chitoi is one kind of cake which is very popular in Bangladesh and West Bengal. It is soft and fluffy. Its shape is round.

4. Chap-dari: It is a specific and popular shape of beard.

5. Mixed savoury snack. Mixed savoury snack is known as chanachur.

Tareq Samin

Sense of Responsibility

Majhar, Santanu and Iqbal were taking tea. Jayanto has yet to come. This roadside tea-stall is their preference. Besides the wide road in this tea-stall, they are the four friends usually pass their time. They are studying M.B.A for a long time, they are the friends to one another.

Majhar is very clever, medium height, slim health, longish face and always in a naughty smile.

Santanu is easy, simple, indifferent in nature. He is the only child of his parents, good health, circle faced. Eyes are bound in the thick-framed spectacle.

Iqbal is a man of poetic and literary flair. With a long slim physique, curly hair, thick eyebrow and something longish face.

In their pastime talk there comes the future scope of jobs, present politics and beautiful girl mates. Most of the time they talk to take these three topics.

Majhar says, 'why Jayanto Saheb is late today?'

'He has some office work today, so he'll be something late today'—Santanu replies.

'After five, why there is an office?'—Iqbal asks to move his eyebrows.

The tea-stall owner Akhtar Mia pouring tea into the kettle remarks, 'people do offices still 10 at night. And he tells why the office is after five? 'Go to do the job you'll understand what would be the matter!'

Majhar sits on the opposite side. He smiles and tells— 'see friends, see behind, your girlfriend is coming.'

To see behind Santanu becomes reddish in shame. A mad, may be between 20 to 30 years old young woman fully naked. Her hair is raveled up. Unclean body, though her body structure is attractive. 'Give money, I'll eat rice?' The mad woman wants alms in a pathetic voice.

In a sense of fear, Santanu leaves his seat and goes away. Now she stretches her hands to Iqbal. 'Why you are rambling without clothes in this way?' Iqbal chides.

Majhar naughtily said, if she would be clothed 'what could you see?'

When Jayanto has come suddenly, nobody knows. He puts off his shirt and gives it to the mad woman's hand. The woman puts on the shirt slowly but surely. He gives a banana and bread to her, as if she is the family member. Eating them the woman happily goes away.

Among them Jayanto is the most neediest and his financial condition is most pathetic. Besides the study, he is doing a job. He sends money to his parents. Though he doesn't miss out the opportunity to help others.

If all the people would be helpful, then all the deprived people of the society could live better. To think this in his mind the tea-stall owner Akhtar Mia releases a big sigh.

Kazi Rafi

The Fire

'Fire', 'Fire', was the only word the old father of a twin daughter had learned to repeat in a reluctant voice in the meantime. There were not any other words than 'fire' that anybody can hear about uttering him at a span of time. So once, he forgot all the words in the world except 'Fire'.

Even though he forgot everything, the words hidden in his heart flowed like a fountain from the top of a high mountain. It's perfect to say those words are not just words but feelings.

He knows not the meaning of those words and doesn't know why those words do not come out with a shape, why those words do not play as a sound throughout the throat naturally. Even he does not know where his thorax generated those words, where the break is, and where they will depart.

Like the repetition of the same feelings of the day in his early life, he first met his eldest daughter, Dola's mother. He wanted to converse with her at length.

Fighting poverty in his childhood and adolescence, he graduated and obtained a job at a major pharmaceutical company in a reduced firefighting position. He finds the first sight of this colourful world of his brutal life in black and white on this day. It seemed that his world had changed.

He got the life with colours, rivers and hills; beneath the soft morning sun, there are playing fresh blooming green cucumbers with pumpkin flowers. There was an indescribable sky, where the grandeur moon-lit night says this life is nothing but an intense mist, in a colourless struggling life who only faced all the points of propensity and the fall of dreams in his way to growing up. He wets his eyes with gratitude to the great creator for making his life so colourful.

Even today, his eyes are getting wet with tears, but he didn't vent a single word from his lips anymore. Can the larynx and lips also be affected by asthma? Due to the asthma disease even drowning in the ocean of air, the lung could not breathe evenly; the air becomes so stingy to it. In the same way, the lips and throat of the older adult-only tremble when they try to act out those inner flows of sound.

But he found the other words again, the day the stranger asked him, "Did you notice any activity of your daughter before she joined IS (Islamic State) in Syria?"

"I... S ... sy... ria?"

"Both your daughters have gone to Syria."

Syria, what is it, why and how it is... Thinking about the word Syria the older man becomes garrulous. His heart becomes anxious with the stranger's words. The stranger repeated to him, "Did you forget the ransom you paid as demanded by kidnapping your two daughters a few days ago? Good god, you are lucky enough, did not pay the whole. ... It is indeed a good ploy of your daughters to fly to Syria. But really, two of your girls were very smart and fast. Spreading the news of their death in a fire, they went to glow the fire in the war in Syria!"

The way his heart was enjoying the moment of his first meeting with Dola's mother, the same feelings besieged him today with replacing the word 'joy' with 'anxiety and extreme 'depression'. Yet, within those words, he sought after a ray of light hint if two of his daughters went to Syria! Then maybe they have survived.

There is nothing better in this beautiful green world than a life in the pink. Every moment of the two sisters growing up from their childhood is projecting quickly like a cinema in his mind. The two of them slept together, ate together, travelled together and participated in various cultural events simultaneously. Ah, those talented, beautiful faces of his daughters, the view of their coiffure ornamented with the Rajanigandha and Palash flowers in spring, now makes him anxious. As if he is enjoying the fragrance of Palash and Shimul flowers of summer times as in his childhood.

And now he sank into another memory. Often, that memory is repeated, pointing fingers to eye him; what a plenary failure man he is. Every moment of the rest of his life may remind him of the fall of his dreams and aspirations.

2

That was a Thursday. A call came to Dola's father's mobile from a shopping store close to the school, "It's better for you to rush to our Agora store next to your daughter's school. She is here in our custody."

"Why, what did she do there?"

"You will see as soon as you arrived."

He is a simple middle-class man. His forehead starts sweating at this slightest threat. His heartbeat sounds rapidly in his ear.

For a lower position staff as a fireman, it was tough to take a short break from duty, and when he got tired to manage his management to allow him a break, again he was called back and told, "you are taking so much time that will force me to give your daughter to the police."

Finally, he rushed to arrive and stopped at the portal of the vast shop. Dola is standing on the side of the counter of the shop with her head bowed down. She holds, hiding something tightly underneath her right-hand fist. One seems to be more interested in the 'piece of her sin` much more than in that hidden object. Males are looking for that signature carves of evil in her growing figure, and women are a quest for it in the beauty of her face soaked in tears. Beauty is the cause of all the sin!

As he climbed only four steps to the carpeted floors of the store, it seems to him to climbing a high hill, a path that never ends. A woman was passing down the stairs, saying, "What a sinister girl! Steals chocolate in a school dress! The images of the school are all gone! Oh, God, how about their parents?"

And just at that moment, his head starts a slight ache. And the world becomes dire before him. He looked around once just before his ears locked. Even all the legs of the mess and all the wheels of all the vehicles are moving, all the words become immobile like wax statues, stagnant and clinging to each other with melted parts. All the sounds, surroundings, and echoes have merged into an invisible world.

At that midday time, the sun is spreading flourishing fire in the sky, yet the crickets are yelling inside his brain, those non-frequency tunes come out from those melted sounds stagnant clinging to each other. Is hiding also a kind of darkness? His eyes behold darkness.

But amid that darkness, the frightened but magical vision of the blurred eyes seemed to save him from falling on the ground. Dola —his eldest daughter. All of the motivation to his triumph to complex works and sweats is Dola. Disgrace and embarrassment in her eyes made him impatient; he ran close to her.

The operator cum manager of the CCTV camera in the shop was closely watching out the girl from a safe distance. They did not allow the girl to move a single step from the point for quite a few hours. Now, finding the girl's father and comes nearer.

"What did she do?"

"What else didn't she do? Paying for a cheap hair clip worth seven bucks only, she left the shop stealing a bar of costly chocolate in her pocket. Even after being caught and asked, but she remained dumb. We have never seen such a masterminded cheat girl of this age! What a thief-girl have you given birth to?"

As if rather than the helplessness of Dola's eyes - filled with tears, their tongues of insulting her father had buried her down in the earth. Her anxious heart tries to imagine that if it may be a moment of the dream or if God would take her back to the classroom as a few hours earlier, she should never come back to this store again. She will never be tempted to have costly chocolate again till her death.

Getting her father's voice, she understood that time has two wings, yet those do not work to fly back. So, as there is no hope to go back to the past and become pure, now she wanted to reach death very fast - the last destination of life with those wings. If those impossible could be turned into possible, that would help Dola to survive with a little more energy. Oh God, let my power of visibility off so that I have not to see my father's shameful and painful eyes!"

And her father said in a low-pitched trembling voice, "sorry, sorry, sir, I will pay for the chocolate. It is not my daughter's fault ... it's mine. She had been asking for a hundred bucks for the chocolate many times, but I could not provide the money to buy her chocolate. All her friends, very often, buy chocolates from here. So ... I'm sorry, really I'm abashed." Saying this, the father looked at his daughter with full of compassion.

At that very precious moment of the father and daughter's conjunction of views, the father noticed that the daughter was anxious to hide her wet cheeks with the chocolate in her fist. She knew not that her hand-held chocolate had been ruined up to ooze.

Although Dola is crying silently, yet it seems the storm flows inside her teenage psyche. As a father, how can he be quiet and calm watching his adolescent daughter's devastation by the storm and he became dumbfounded, thinking that how he would be able to save his two daughters in this ocean of lousy time?

This society! Society only stands on the scales of measuring sin and virtue only in the eyes of the law. They are not towards children's humanity, younger and helpless, but towards those who can show thumbs to this law; they can pressurize those scales.

The store manager said, "A rubbish daydreamer! No cost to say sorry! Don't cry over spilt milk now. What will I do with your sorry! Ashamed! Don't be fake ashamed. You are trying to pay for the price of chocolate only, it will not do, and you will have to pay the fine for the crime she committed here."

With a foggy vision of his eyes, Dolar's father made a strange calculation of his life while paying a hundred taka for his daughter's chocolates and another one thousand taka as a fine. If he had spent five hundred taka for his daughter's wishes before, he might not have felt so ashamed today.

Her father holds her by the hand on the way back home; saying nothing to her but himself, he whispered, 'death is better than insult.' And just then, he remembered the view of a Krishnacura tree standing for a long time on the bank of a dry river passing through the village. Maybe God is giving him a hint. He said to Dola, "Baby, you won't tell your mother anything about this incident. And yes, a piece of good news for you, we will go to our village with you all next week on holiday. There at the bank of the river, in the rain-soaked green, there is now Krishnacura blossom-like fire. You are also as beautiful as those flowers, my heart."

3.

The visitant was vexed, "Hey uncle, what's wrong with you? Why you are not saying anything?"

Today, the memory of the beautiful fire red Krishnacura ignited a new fire to the soft, fresh, and green memories of the father. After a long recess, he returned to reality. The mysterious stranger looked deep into the father's eyes. It seems as if a flame of fire from the man's heart was reflecting on his facial manifestations.

As soon as he felt, the heart of the father burst into tears at the insecurity of the spirits of the damsels burnt in the fire. He said, "Impossible. My daughters and others of my family were pure religious practice, but no one has the mentality to be orthodox.

"Many girls went, and a few are going to Syria that time; Referring to them, once my younger daughter said, 'Why these girls are so bullshit? In the sight of Allah, they two are not equal: they who can see and those who cannot see having two eyes. They are so blind!"

"But they can change their mind?"

"You're doing something wrong. Don't impose such a big slander on my daughters, young man." He tendriled the stranger's hand impatiently.

"Two of my daughters stopped at a shop just to buy some cheap ornaments on their way back home after singing on a patriotic stage program. They told me over the phone that they would return shortly after. You may check out my call list!"

"Look at these pictures..."

Then with the photo evidence, the stranger gave a detailed description of how the two girls went to Syria from that shop.

Dola's father, with his astonished eyes, looked at the newcomer young man; kept looking. And availing the ability to ask a question, "Who are you, how it is possible for you to know so many details! But two years back, who raped my eldest daughter, yet nobody can find them out! Do you know the details? can you show me in detail like this one, please?"

"Oh, so...? I guess they took up arms to pay off that."

"Those who can sing such a patriotic song so passionately - they can't take up arms in hand."

"Soil, time, and society have all changed. Now no artist, teacher-professor, doctor-engineer, a businessman can be trusted," said the visitor.

Dola's father marked that though the stranger mentioned many classes of people but avoided the government officials and forces who are mostly corrupted. He took out a part of Dola's burnt veil from the pocket of his dirty Panjabi. Today he found a fire burning again in the maroon-green Georgette veil. The older man's mirthless vision getting narrowed. In his spirit, the guilt of not protecting the memory of the girl in his soul, his heart wanted to protest so strongly in all the known and unknown languages of the world that this time he even forgot the word 'fire'.

The antagonism speeding from the heart to speed up the blood circulation in his body hit his brain in the wrong way.

The half-burnt veil is yet burning by the perfunctory fire. The father looked at it and asked himself silently why it was the fire when it was born; he has forgotten all about it. And it became his destiny to be fastened in the memory of the DNA- the sentient nervous system of a human species billions of years ago and to lie remain in bed.

Now a scene floats in his mind, a group of cannibals from the un-civilised era, naked and half-naked people, is swallowing non-burned meat in front of the cave by lighting a fire in his daughter's veil!

Translated by Ashraf-ul Alam Shikder

Ashraf-ul Alam Shikder

Scribe

On a beautiful morning, Kanu is unable to rise as early as he always does. His eyes awakened around 8:00 a.m., but he didn't pick up his right hand, so he couldn't get out of bed at that time. Kanu, Kamal Hossain Kanu. Nowadays, he is a pretty well-sold-out author. Because the university is not in session these days, he is taking advantage of the time to write more short stories for his next book.

Publishers are putting money aside for his book. Even the editors - sub-editors - ask him for the material regularly. He no longer contributes stories to any low-circulation periodicals, small magazines, or online publications. The secret behind the fact is just known by his wife only -he has bound to let her know, they do need not spend any single paisa from his salary he gets from the University of Dhaka; She is proud of herself as the finest cook and the non-metric wife of the writer husband.

However, every dog has a bad day. 'Doesn't worry, you only need three months to restore and a psychotherapist for regular exercise,' says the doctor, who prescribed him a few drugs after certain tests.

'Doctor, please tell me what made me crippled?'

'It was a mild stroke, but it could turn into a major one that takes your life. Please refrain from smoking.'

Kanu, for the first time, prays to Allah and feels thankful for his life. Now that his writing career is in ruins; he thinks about his wife instead of his hand, but she, despite her fondness for the scheme, dismisses it. Kanu was furiously formulating his schemes in this respite helplessly, and on those days, Ritu, one of his students, volunteered to offer him a long sitting every day for the benefit of Bengali literature. Because She is also a student of Bengali literature.

Ritu is the most methodical; her handwriting is so beautiful that it could be described as calligraphic. She learned and experienced that an appealing bad girl - student with good handwriting does not need to study all year. Even in life, there was no inconvenience. She realized there must be a wealthy and obnoxious husband waiting for her.

She began writing as our author was creating his story, and she continued. As a result, they finish the first one and move on to the next, and the next, and the next, and so on, until they've established a specific system for their creative writing.

The first written story was published within one week after finishing the story. The fact makes them cheerful, even Kanu's wife. But she became jubilant just after receiving a cheque from the publisher of the magazine. Ritu was invited by the Mrs. writer for dinner that night.

Television was swapped the time of reading in middle-class family lives. Even everybody at Ritu's residence in Faridpur, and in Dhaka the family of her maternal aunty in their government quarter read the story and feels like a part of their own life.

Her boyfriend kissed her saying, 'Middle-aged men are very salacious.'

'Jealous?'

'Everyone saying, you did it for your exam.'

'Yes.'

'It's easy to say, but hard to listen.'

'So sweet of you…'

Then Ritu left for the shower.

Farhod Eshanov

Brunette and Blonde

Every time before her, the aroma of hot cappuccino filled the room.

Because she had a great interest in the piles of crumpled papers that were scattered everywhere in my room, the antediluvian typewriter on my desk, and the garish writing on the edge of the machine, she never forgot to bring a fortified drink in the morning. Her daily habits managed to become an integral part of my life. The round trace of a plastic cup here on the table, though I tried all night to make my manuscripts a mess, was put down by her in an hour and sitting on a chair by the window, with a quiet voice she read what I wrote during the night… All this repeats in a trace. And I wake up, not refraining from the smell of the invigorating drink. Without lifting my head from the table, with the outside of my palm I touch the cup and wait for it to cool. When did that smell become native to me?

I wonder if I'll ever get tired of that smell, that story, starting from my doorstep to the table, her tickling my nasopharynx!

Then her tinkling laughter reached me bookended my thoughts, which had no time to leave the outside universe, flying away like smoke, occupying my being.

– Tell me the reason you laughed, Aurora?

To avoid seeing her mocking gaze, without opening my eyes from the glass I held in my hand.

– Ah, Osvaldo, Osvaldo! – She went on in an interesting and pleasant voice. – It turns out you have a great sense of humour!

I didn't know that... because until now, I've known you as a writer who describes negative feelings, emotions and mental anguish. Apparently, today I reinvented you for myself.

The amazement in her eyes didn't try to stop for one minute. I was already beginning to worry, not from the fact that she was laughing, not understanding the meaning of my lines, but from her incessant laughter.

In spite of my rage, I did not jump to conclusions. On the contrary, I preferred to observe Aurora's pure laughter. As if I understood that even brunette bodies can tweak the sun's rays, I took my gaze away from her beautiful swarthy neck.

Fortunately, she didn't have time to notice as the phone rang.

– Yes, madam. Here I am, reading your son's new story. You won't believe it, but the subject of his next story... Mmm... Yes, yes, I've already done everything... Yes, like you said... Okay, I'll tell him...

She hung up.

– Your mother called. She absolutely resisted your writing. And also... she told you not to bother.

Aurora wanted to reflect her shock at her and got agitated. It seemed to me as if she was mumbling. Soon she began to prepare the medicine I was to take. The mere thought of having to swallow the hateful pills made me cringe all over. I crumpled my cup in anger and tossed it into the basket in the corner of the room, where the crumpled container sat next to yesterday's cups. It seemed to me that this routine would last forever.

– It amazes me that you couldn't take even one step out of the house and how you write about the beauty of sea breezes, azure shores? You portray as if you had been and lived there all your life. I'm very curious to know who the beautiful Margo? – Suddenly she asked the question, forwarding the medicine with water.

And I continued to retell what I had put into lines yesterday.

– There was no prettier girl on the coast than she was. People streaming in from the surrounding area were struck by her beauty, sometimes at a loss for words. Her snow-white smile and graceful sophistication drove many men mad. However, her soul was pure and clear as the night moon, which illuminated the dark surface of the sea.

As the night moon rises in the sky, you can watch her move smoothly across the sea to the shore. The sparkling sparks on the moon's surface give joy to the eyes and peace to the soul. And I sat on the coastal sands, surrendering to sad thoughts. How could I not react to the whistling, the excessive attention to her person when she was followed by glances and compliments.

And then I began to wonder: since when did I become interested in the antics of these people? I remembered those days with regret. It was only Margo's beautiful voice that brought me to my senses, relieving me of all sorts of thoughts.

"Excuse me, sir…"

At first, her slender legs appeared before my eyes, which delighted the eye and excited the blood…

Out of surprise, I was speechless. And she went on, as if to say she was here.

– Sir, my name is Margherita Berardi. If you don't mind, I'll keep you company and we'll talk," she chirped, bringing me to my senses.

– Of course, please… – I said kindly, which was very uncharacteristic of me…

A smile appeared on Aurora's frozen face again. And with even more enthusiasm she began to ask questions.

-Ah, my dear Osvaldo, could you… could you do such… It's hard to believe…

Aurora's interest in this story was growing by the minute. I realized that I would only be free of her inquiries if I told her the whole story.

– Aurora, I wasn't always in this position…

Her eyes opened wide, as if she did not recognize me. Apparently, my companion thought that I had been so helpless and pathetic all my life…

– Those legs weren't always as paralyzed as they are now… I'll tell you… This weak body became so not so long ago… I'm not congenitally disabled…

Today, my maid turned into a listening ear: she listened to every word I said with great interest. Because she was thrilled to hear from the author himself, who had been a burden to his mother all his life, being bedridden inside four walls, had always been in no such position had seen the days in his youth.

– That day we sat next to Margo on the beach. Our heartfelt, sincere conversation seemed to last an eternity. Those were the most beautiful moments. And then...

– And then... then you liked each other... – Aurora finished for me, as if she was previously aware of the meaning of my story.

– Yes, we liked each other... – I confirmed her assumption.

I did not dare to tell Aurora about unforgettable impressions of that one night spent with Margo, so I was not ashamed. No wonder she'd had enough of the way I reflected on the past, staring at the ceiling. She realized long ago that I should be left alone with these memories. Aurora is the maid my mother hired to serve me, for six years she has managed to occupy a place in my soul. And she is a very perceptive woman. It's not for nothing that I consider her an integral part of my life. However, she seemed noble and charming at that moment my thoughts were occupied only with Margo. Her beautiful voice rang in my ears...

"My dear Osvaldo, those beautiful moments spent with you I will remember all my life. You opened your soul to me. Your generosity will seal itself in my heart. I will never regret handing over my soul. I will look forward to the day when fate will bring us together again. Farewell, Osvaldo, farewell!"

– That day, as she uttered these parting words, she thought I was not yet awake. As she tried to leave the hut, she looked in my direction one last time. And we never saw each other again, our paths parted…

At one point I was crippled: what was so funny about the story Aurora found in my story that I had been writing all night. Why was she laughing? No matter how hard I tried to find an answer to that question, I couldn't. Certainly, she is a good reader. I thought she was laughing at the inaccuracy of the writing.

– Mr. Osvaldo, -Aurora turned to me, having finished her work and going home.

I looked back in her direction. It turned out that up to now I had never had to walk my maid to the door. I remembered this as she put on her slippers.

Aurora looked in my direction. When she saw that I was looking at her, she froze in an instant. Thus, we gazed at each other for a long time, while discomfort appeared between us. And to get rid of the discomfort, I said:

– All right, go…

– Goodbye, sir…

– See you…

All night I tried to remember the moments in my life that were worth remembering. To be precise, my memory flashed back to that one night with Margo and the six-year experience of living with Aurora. It's hard to make a final decision between erratic thoughts.

However, I was clearly aware that I needed to confess my feelings to Aurora. Although I noticed sincerely that she loved me too, I was afraid of her reaction-she might leave me forever if I told her of my love. If there was such a possibility, she would have left long ago. She hadn't missed a day of work in those six years. Surely Aurora is worthy of my love. Tomorrow, yes, yes, tomorrow I'll tell you that...

Favourite smell of cappuccino- Without opening my eyes, I touched the glass with one hand. The temperature is just right. No familiar silhouette near the window, however. Strangely, the papers scattered around the room were not put away. In the kitchen, an unfamiliar girl. I turned the stroller in her direction.

– Are you awake?

This girl, who looked like Aurora, was about sixteen years old. But why isn't she here? Why didn't she come? These questions were keeping me awake...

– Yes, Aurora... -Before I could finish my question, she sensitively continued my words.

– Sir, I am Aurora's daughter. My mother sent you this and told me to tell you that she won't be able to come here anymore… We warned your mother. From tomorrow you will have a new maid…

Hearing this girl's words made my insides burn. It seemed that my story flashed before my eyes again, as if they had been healthy for me. And now a letter and a book wrapped in paper lay before me…

"My dear Osvaldo forgive me. I quit my job because I can no longer hide my love. Yesterday before I left, I saw you looking at me intently, and I was aware that you too were beginning to have feelings for me. At first, I rejoiced considerably. After all, I had waited six years for this day. But, after reading your last story, I finally realized that it was all wrong. And I, the fool, couldn't close my eyes, knowing everything. Do you remember that I laughed when I read your story? Then I actually cried inside. When I found out that you still loved Margo, I couldn't stop myself. And when you were near me, I consciously pretended to laugh…

And the reason why we can no longer meet you, you will know when you open the paper. I hope it will be the best birthday present ever. I hope to see you soon. Aurora…"

My eyes filled with tears; I didn't have the courage to drop them. It was certain that this gift, the book. But now, what book would soften the present situation? I angrily began to tear off the cover.

On the cover of the book was written – "Oswald". The author was Marguerite Berardi.

Akhtar Hossain

She Was A Virgin

The bus dropped him off near the end of the village—strange name for a village—Solitude! Strange but eerily appropriate, so it seemed to Rob. There seemed to be no human being around. Those that were around did not seem to be alive. The birds did not seem to know how to sing. The river did not seem to have its natural flow anywhere. A thick blanket of silence seemed to reign all around. It is not just the end of the village; it is the end of the world, thought Rob. As the bus roared down the hills out of his sight it seemed like falling off the edge of the earth into an eternity of void and emptiness.

Rob took his first cautious step onto the soil of this strange land—the soil that did not seem to be trodden before. As earth that was rusting away for lack of human touch; a bunch of tender green grass caressing his feet—grass that just work up at the gentle touch of his shoes.

Rob took out a piece of paper from his pocket. Everything seemed to be in order. This was the beginning of the last leg of his journey—Destination: "the House of the Police Inspector."

After Rina was married off to an unknown man of an unknown place Rob found no reason to stick around in his old village. She was the love of his life, his only love. So, he moved to the city where he was met with a life of utter loneliness and chronic unemployment. He did not like the city, but there was nowhere he could go back to. There was no one to share his life, his moments of joy or his moments of despair. A life without Rina was a life without a sense of anything. He had no feelings, no wish, and no desire. He had just one obligation—an obligation to live out his wretched life somehow. Only if he had a bit of money in his hands he could afford to be as reckless with his life as he wanted. But you cannot be reckless with an empty pocket—not in a cruel town. It is at that desperate time of his life that this unusual ad in the paper caught his eye "Young man/woman to take care of an eighty-year-old lady; Twenty-four hours all-inclusive personal service; Heavy monetary compensation guaranteed." It seemed pretty attractive to him. He went for the interview which was held in the same town. Young or old, what did he care! He was not one to spend much time or thought on his career. He had nothing to lose. Naturally, the interview went quite well. He landed the job.

The first stop was supposed to be the House of the Police Inspector where he was to report his arrival. Then someone from the House was supposed to lead him to the top of a hillock in a tree-shaded little cottage called the "Solitary Villa." Rob remembers the puzzled look on the face of his fellow passenger on the bus when he mentions his destination. "God be with you, young man," is how the man started. Then a chilling description of what had happened to the village to earn its distinctive name¾the very mention of the two words. Inspector House can freeze a person out of his wits. The trees can shed their leaves, the river can reverse its flow and the infants can stop sucking the mother's breast. The name of the tyrant was Inspector Alim. Tasiran Bibi is the present occupant of the Solitary Villa. Rob's ward-to-be, was his eldest daughter. Such a beastly bull he was that in his presence a village-full of peasants would seem like a row of corpses waiting to be buried. Legend has it that once a goat in his herd of animals died. The whole village had to mourn its death. It was not an ordinary goat¾it was Inspector Alim's goat. There is no end of legends in his name.

There was just one chair on the front porch. Rob stood beside it and glanced around his surroundings. There was an over-possessing sense of silence everywhere. There were some signs of human habitation but no real life anywhere. Presently came two huge men carrying on their shoulders a very old man from inside the house¾a house that had all the outward signs of wealth and prosperity. The old man seemed to have only one half of his body alive and mobile and the other half dead and still. The two men seated him on the chair and stood back in grim silence with their hands clasped over their chest as if to guard the two halves of the master's body.

A little fly was buzzing around for a while that Rob could not help noticing. Suddenly it decided to settle on the cheek of the old man. Rob took an immediate liking for the little creature¾this was the only thing that seemed to be cheerfully alive in that God-forsaken place. Unfortunately, however, one of the two attendants immediately pounced on the poor fly, squeezed it in his hand and threw it in the burning fire inside an urn by the chair. The ferocity of the whole exercise was impressive indeed, a stark reminder that this is the house of the infamous Inspector. It also became clear to Rob that he was standing in front of Inspector Nasir, the youngest son of Inspector Alim.

Soon somebody came to take Rob to the "Solitary Villa" —a small cottage that stood on the top of a hill at the end of the village that Rob thought was the end of the world. Perhaps the most desolate place in the whole universe. A large old Shimool tree was blocking the hot sun away from the cottage in which lay the old dame Tasiran Bibi, who seemed to have nothing in life but to wait for the last call from her Creator. She was not allowed in the main house down the valley because of a deadly disease that she was supposed to have contacted from somewhere, that was slowly shedding her flesh away from her fingers and destroying the pigment of her skin. It was believed to be highly contagious. Nobody wanted the job of caring for the old lady. There were two women and three men who came at various times to look after her, but they all left at the first opportunity they got. They still couldn't escape the worse. They all died under mysterious circumstances—two by drowning, one by asphyxiation, and the other two were stabbed to death. All by the hand of phantom power, people say. Inspector Nasir warned him about it and had him wear a good-luck bead on his arm to ward off the ghosts. The man who accompanied him to the cottage left without a single word. Not even when Rob asked him a pointed question. As if he had lost his tongue.

Sheepishly Rob entered the room. Nobody came to clean the room for three full days. Human excrement was littered everywhere. The Bibi was continuously talking to herself while Rob was trying hard to keep from throwing up. As soon as she felt the presence of a stranger in the room she started screaming obscenities at him—"Who are you? What the hell do you think you are doing in my room? Are you like those suckers who came to rob me and starve me to death? Are you going to starve me also?" Rob felt like running away from that miserable place, this miserable person. But then he calmed down, put a piece of cloth on his nose, held his ground, and shouted back at the lady—"Why on earth are you screaming like that? Don't you see I am a new man on the job? Let me have a look at this horrible mess you have created here."

Nobody ever talked back to the daughter of Inspector Alim in this insolent manner. She got furious ¾"How dare you boy. How dare you talk to me like that?" Not to be undone by her fury he shot back ¾"Don't call me a boy. Then I'll go on calling you a girl." Bibi was so stunned she was at a loss to say anything more.

But it was not insolence or insubordination that drove him to say those awful things that he said to the lady. It was just that he was so anxious to bring back a semblance of life to this place. He was deliberately trying to provoke her to respond to a situation that she never had to encounter before. Besides, since he decided to keep the job he wanted to make this place as livable as possible and as quickly as possible. So, he got down to the business of clearing it up, faeces and all, with his bare hands. And in no time the job was done. The room never looked as clean as it looked now. Even the ever-irritable Bibi could not help noticing, but she was not the one to give in so easily. She kept on screaming insults at him that he thought best to ignore. Soon she would calm down and learn to accept the new reality of life and accept it gracefully. There was no clear winner in the first around of their battle of nerves but the advantage seemed to be leaning towards Rob.

Bibi was clearly all of her eighty-long years, in body and spirit. Her skin was nothing but a knot of wrinkles, like the body of a crocodile. Her hair reminded him of the woolly feathery plant that grew in the fields of his village. Rob was preparing to give her a full bath. He boiled a bucketful of water, as she wanted. He would have to place her on a metal chair before pouring water on her. But first, he thought he should take the heavy robe off her body and place thin light apparel on her. All of a sudden, the whole world seemed to fall apart in front of his eyes. He was not going to believe what he saw. How many unbelievable wonders are there in the world? This has to top all of them. Underneath the neckline of that frail body, below that surface that was exposed to the human eye laid another world, another body, the body of a sixteen-year-old girl with all its peaks and curves, all the sparkling texture of a smooth silvery soft skin. Is it how the body of a sweet-sixteen really looks like? Rob would not know. Rina, his lost love was not as sweet and her body was not so smooth. Rob kept looking at her in utter amazement. On one side of the body, it is the crocodile skin, and a full-blown river on high tide on the other. The earth seemed to have erupted under his feet. The sun touched down on his head.

There was no wish in his life that Rob had left any urge to fulfil. But he certainly wanted to uncover this mystery. How could a sixteen-year-old girl still live in the body of an eighty-year-old woman? Rob knew it would not be easy to pry out the secret from her, so he started working is charm on her. Sweet talk, flattery, efficient service finally won her over. One day she poured her heart out to him, something that she never did to anyone before.

The young man's name was Ali. She was madly in love with him, and he with her. They belonged to each other. She was still in her teens. A sweet-sixteen, brimming with the youthful exuberance of life ready to live or die for the love of her life. One moonlit night, under a tall Banyan tree, in an exquisitely romantic setting, they met, for the first time, to share the forbidden fruit. She was going to let him explore her body—discover all of her peaks and valleys, crooks and corners, caves and crests. It would be like a sacred offering to her God. In a moment of supreme ecstasy, he was standing there with his eyes closed, anticipating the world of joy that he was going to enter. Then, suddenly like the crackle of thunder from a clear blue sky, came down a bunch of armed men who worked for her father. They did not say anything, did not ask anything. In one lethal stroke of a machete, they dislodged Ali's head from his body. Right in front of her horrified eyes, the body dropped on the ground like a sack of flour. They were not finished yet. They cut up the whole body into small pieces and spread it across an elevated wooden board so that the crows and vultures can enjoy a good meal. From that day no one could ever touch her body. She vowed not to let anyone see what was beyond her neckline, not even the birds or the sun, the moon or the air. She vowed not to speak to anyone about it, not to mention to anyone what happened on that fateful night. For long sixty-plus years she kept her word. She kept herself locked in this horrible cage called the Solitary Villa, just to avoid contact with the animals of the big house, her father and all the rest of them. The shouts and screams and obscenities are all a charade, just to keep them at bay, to keep anyone from getting close to her. But who are you, young man? How could you break that wall of mine? How could you trick into breaking my vow?

Yes, he did and he did not know how. Perhaps no one was as gentle with her as Rob was. Perhaps no one wanted to hear her story as much as he did. Whatever the reason he was deeply moved. He was on the verge of tears; he couldn't speak for a while.

At night, Bibi was sleeping in her room and Rob in his. Suddenly Rob woke up in the middle of the night, as if in pain or from a nightmare. A sense of deep sadness for Bibi descended within his heart; a surge of great compassion for the broken woman. Despite all the awful things that have happened to her, her body is still one of the greatest wonders of the world. Two women in one body—one is eighty and the other still sixteen. The sixteen-year-old is still waiting to be touched, to be hugged, to be loved. As if she was still hoping that one day the spirit of Ali will rise above the mist of time and free her body from the agony of living without him. Could it be that Rob is really not the same Rob that he was before, but the spirit of Ali?

Stealthily he opened Bibi's door knowing quite well what a slight sleeper she was. Maybe he would take her head on his lap and tell the story of his own life, of Rina, of his broken heart in a moonlit night. But Bibi was in deep sleep, for a change. He took her head on his lap but she wouldn't wake up. Suddenly a strange feeling came upon him; and he became oblivious of time and space. Was it Bibi or Rina? Was it his hand that was reaching down the curves and valleys of the body hunting for treasure in a mysterious land? He was in a trance. He was unable to control his own movements. Down the wavy lines of that wonderfully luscious body his fingers reached that heavenly river, that land of magical bliss. As if his whole body caught in fire. He was being swept away by a storm of unimaginable power. He had reached the zenith of raw human passion.

The following day Rob was going to give her a bath. He boiled a bucket of water, as usual, kept the metal chair in place for her to sit on and reached out for her robe. Then, suddenly, yet another wonder flashed in front of his eyes. It was not the same body anymore. It was not the same enchanting world that he let himself run rampant in last night. Her body came back to the eighty-year-old dame Bibi, Inspector Alim's spinster daughter. The spirit of Ali had seemed to depart at long last. She broke loose from the tyranny of that ghostly moonlit night sixty-four years ago, but alas! This is not what Rob wanted to see. He did not want to see the full river dried up in one night. He did not want to see the crocodile claim her entire body. Thanks to him she had lost her chastity, so he thought. The virginity that she had preserved for all those years had finally been compromised by what must have been his unbecoming conduct of last night. He had robbed her of her crown jewel, the treasure that she had kept unseen and untouched just so that she could offer it at the altar of her God of love.

Having attended to all the needs of Bibi, Rob got out of the villa to take a seat under the big shimool tree. A deep sense of remorse and regret was tormenting him inside. He took a fallen branch of the tree that had more thorns than leaves. He started hitting the hand that soiled the sacred body last night. The more he hit the more enraged he got. He started screaming to the wilderness, to the sky above, to the tree—"But she was a virgin, she was a virgin." His anguish was unbelievable. He was losing control.

The following day there was a rumour in the village that the ghost of the Shimool-tree had claimed Rob's life. They all came to see with their own eyes. And they all saw what they heard. His body was hanging from a string tied to an upper branch of the tree. Nothing out of the ordinary as far as the villagers are concerned, except Rob's hand that was bleeding profusely.

Everything was eerily quiet again—the people, the wind, the tree, the birds and the river, except the dame Bibi—" I am hungry" she said, "aren't you going to give me anything to eat?"

Aporanho Shushmito

Neligan or Aporanho

I grew up in Goalbathan, Gopalganj, in a Christian missionary ashram. While in a missionary school, Father Gilbert called me one day and told me everything. According to the registrar's book, my date of birth is 29th February. Father said that one of the local fisherwomen left me at this ashram on a stormy night. My baptism was performed through a small ceremony.

They documented Sheikh Mujibur Rahman as my father. When father of the Nation Bangabandhu announced:
From today, the name of the father of all the orphans in Bangladesh should be named after him.
Honouring that announcement, Father Gilbert made me the son of Bangabandhu and showed the sign of infinite compassion.

The rules and regulations of the ashram were very strict. We were a Christian community believing in The Seventh Day Adventist. I would go to church every Saturday morning and prayed with our closed eyes.

"And the dragon was wroth with the woman and went to make war with the remnant of her seed, which keeps the commandments of god, and have the testimony of Jesus Christ."

A couple from Montreal, Canada once visited Gopalganj and came to our ashram. They spent the entire day with us, talking, taking pictures. When they were about to leave in the evening, I held the hand of the lady very tight as if I would not let her go.

The French couple became exceedingly emotional. Upon going back to Canada, they filed the application to adopt me. I moved to Montreal with them. The couple had a son and a daughter of their own. However, a new problem was raised with me. Despite trying hard, I was not speaking. I would spend days holding onto the hands of my mom, but I would not say a word.

They took me to paediatricians, speech therapists and many more, but there was no improvement. They examined me and couldn't find any issues. I still did not speak; I did not learn the language. My adopted parents were very sad.

When I was 8 years old, I suddenly started talking. Usually, the little ones say a word or two, but I started saying the whole sentence at once.

My parents named me Emil Neligan. Named after a famous Quebec poet. When the snow covered all the windows in our city, I started writing poems with my nose in the book.

I have never been good at studies, but somehow, I still finished college.

On a beautiful flowery autumn morning, I lost both my parents in a horrible road accident. I was diagnosed with schizophrenia right after. I wrote countless poems on the windowsill, on the market bill, on my girlfriend's bare back.

When my condition worsened, I was re-admitted to Douglas Mental Hospital.

One time I rushed to Bangladesh on a whim. I came to Gopalganj and started looking for my birth mother. When an illustrated report about me was published in 'Prothom Alo', I found my birth mother in a supernatural steamer! It was a wonderful watershed event.

I am in Madhabpur tea garden since the day before yesterday. My mother is a tea garden labour. She lives in an almost dark skull of a slum. In the evenings, she drinks and mutters unknown words. I don't understand her, but I realise the root of my schizophrenic attacks. I can feel it's coming back.

As I start to spend sleepless nights, I murmured French poetry in the moonlit green woods of Madhabpur. Before the hallucinations begin, I start taking Epival and Closaril.

The moon comes down like on the watershed, within the reach of my hands. I gazed and saw the unworldly moonlight like a dazzling cockatoo. The shimmering reflection of the moon, on the top of the tea leaves at the side of the sloping hill. My eyes get moist. My labour mother goes out there to look for me. I hear her intoxicated anxious call. Calling in her local odd tune.

- "Hey Emil. Hey Niligan … where did you go? Snakes will bite you … Hey, can you hear me?..what is that sound? will you respond??"

I weep holding the branches of the tea tree all alone. I keep muttering.

"Mama, je ne suis pas Nelligan. Je suis Aporanho. (Mom, I'm not Emil Neligan, I am Aporanho ..)"

Note:
Ashram - Hermitage

Translated by Momo Quazi

AKM Abdullah

The Nail of Time

Alam has been in jail for a long time. Luckily, there is only one prisoner named Basir with him in a small room. Alam seems a lot tired lately.

After turning off the lights at night, Bashir heard the sound of crying. Bashir doesn't know much about Alam. But he saw most of the time Alam stay quiet and looked polite in jail.

Alam has worked hard inside the jail all day today. He was very tired; therefore, Alam didn't talk with Bashir at night. Lying down in exhaustion. Drowning into a deep sleep.

Suddenly Alam's eyes fell on the front door. The door is the grill of their room. He saw Surma coming towards Alam with a bag of grilled kebab. Surma dressed up the way she dressed on her wedding day. She wears the last Valentine's gift given by Alam which was a white sari with a red border. Alam's favourite lipstick is also applied to the lips. Alam's nose was hit by the familiar perfume and the sweet scent of Surma's body. Alam happily got up to go towards Surma. He became anxious to hug her. He loves Surma more than his life. Alam has endured many insults for loving Surma. After going through many ups and downs, one day the two got married. Slowly Alam started walking towards the grill. Surma has already come to the grill. Alam extended his arms towards Surma. Surma also extended her hand towards Alam. Alam hugged Surma and in a trembling voice say Surma- Surma…

Suddenly the jailer's stick hit the grill. Alam fell to the floor and his wet eyes saw the stained walls of the small room inside the jail. Surma's bloody body floated through the darkness of the forest and in his hand, was that wheel spanner.

Eity Mithila

Think Before You Bring A New Life

One afternoon, I felt so hungry and mom wasn't at home.
Thought "why not going outside and buy a burger?"
I locked our flat and went outside. While placing order
in a burger shop, I felt something pulling my dress from
behind. Turning back, I saw a little girl.
What happened? I asked.
She with fear replied,"please buy me something to eat
sis, I haven't eat anything today"
There was rush, I couldn't hear her properly, so placing
order I took her to a calm place nearby.
"What's your name?" I asked
"Ranu"she replied with a trembling tone.
"Ok now say Ranu why are you begging and where is
your parents?"I asked.
Sis we don't have our father with us, he has married
other women and doesn't give us anything now"she
replied with tears in eyes.
"Where is your mother then?" I asked.
Mother is sick doing hard work to manage our food and
now I and my brother manage food by begging.
"So you don't go to school?" I asked
She ironically replied,"No food in stomach and you are
asking about school!"
Then I told her to call her brother who was somewhere
nearby that place begging.

After a while she returned with her brother, wearing a old torn lungi sometimes covering uper part of his body and sometimes lower, whispering his sister"will this lady buy us food sis?"

Avoiding his question Ranu told me," sis it's my bother,farid"

I asked farid,"what would you like to eat?"

Hearing this words he became restless to choose what to take from the food carts nearby.

I was following them wherever they were moving.

At a time,farid stopped in front of a food cart pointing his finger to a big pan frying chicken.

"Sister I would like to have it"He told me.

The seller was scolding farid and ranu as he knows they have no money to buy.

Then I came to the front and told him,"give them food, I will pay".

Seller then asked them to stand quite and not to touch anything.

Ranu and farid was standing like statue as the seller told.

Paying for food I moved to my way to take my burger and was noticing them from a bit far how happy they were getting food.

While returning home I was looking in the sky often with deep long breath leaving out with profound hate for that man who had brought these innocent souls to this world. He shouldn't bring any life if he can't keep them happy.

Everyone should think 100 times before taking any decision when other lives are involved with them.

Roksana Lais

Similarity

Ma asks the maid's name. She's a newcomer, a young girl, maybe 10 or 11 years old. She arrived from the village with a cloth sack in her hand. The girl silently stands in front of Ma with a shy disposition. The guard from the front door brought her inside and went back to his work – she's a distant relative of his. With her uncle leaving her on her own among a group of strangers, it seems as if she has accidentally fallen into the ocean. After some time of being asked, the girl finally, slowly says her name is Sara. Ma immediately responds, "well we can't call you by that name, Sara is my daughter's name. We'll have to give you a new name". Ma doesn't even take two minutes to think, she gives the girl a new name, as if she already knew from before the girl arrived, that she would need a new name. "Your name is Tuni, from today onwards when you hear the name 'Tuni', you'll know that you're being called. Will you remember that?" Ma asks the girl. The girl hasn't spoken a word other than having said her name. She continues to stand there with her head hung low. All of us standing in front of her, are all brand-new strangers to her; Dad, Ma, Brother, Sister, the driver and I. But no one asks her how she's feeling about meeting all these new people – whether that's something she's okay with, something she accepts. Ma asks her over and over whether she'll remember her new name, 'Tuni'. She tilts her head up and down to indicate that she'll remember but doesn't actually say anything. She quietly continues to stand in the same position, completely silent. Ma takes her and goes towards the kitchen. The girl named Sara spends many years of her life at our house under the name Tuni. At first, Ma couldn't stand her. Ma always worried whether she would steal food and eat it, whether she would steal food and keep it in her cloth sack. So, Ma always kept a watchful eye on her. Many times, Ma would open Tuni's sack to make sure nothing had been stolen. If Tuni didn't do her work the way she was shown, Ma would slap her now and again. Ma would also always live in fear of when Tuni might run away. What a predicament, fearing Tuni might steal, yet keeping her as a maid due to needing someone to do the housework, while also being anxious that she may flee. After spending many years having these hesitations and worrisome thoughts, at some point, Ma finally decided that Tuni wouldn't steal or run away. In fact, Ma's belief in Tuni grew. Ma has spent a lot of time comfortably living her life since letting go of her hesitations and allowing the girl named Sara who became Tuni to take care of all the household work. At one point when Tuni got older, Ma herself arranged Tuni's marriage. Now Tuni comes to visit us now and then with her husband and children. When Tuni comes to our house, Tuni does the cooking and feeds everyone, as if Tuni has come back to her own family home. When I first enrolled in university, I really liked a teacher of mine. A young woman, who I immediately grew a liking for from the first moment I saw her. I decided I want to do my work-study assignment under her. Her name is Sara, just like mine. I'm Sara Samia, her name is Sara Habib, our old maid's name is also Sara, but she didn't have a last name. There were seven of us who decided to do our work-study assignment under Sara Samia. However, one this particular day, I went by myself to see her to understand the assignment more clearly. She greeted me very cheerfully and explained the assignment to me really well. As I packed up my things and was getting ready to leave, she said to me, "don't introduce yourself as 'Sara' at university anymore, use the name 'Samia' instead. In fact, don't ever tell anyone else at university that your name is Sara". I felt deeply angry. Many of my friends already call me Sara, they can't just start calling me Samia now, that doesn't make any sense. Why do I have to hide my name being Sara? I leave feeling annoyed.

A long time ago, a girl named Sara had her name changed to 'Tuni' at our house. That image floats in my mind. Suddenly I really wanted to know how Tuni felt when her name was changed. At my next lecture with Professor Sara Habib, before I've had a chance to tell anyone about what she had said to me about changing my name, she tells the whole class to call me Samia instead of Sara from now on. She proceeds to keep calling me Samia over and over. Even if Samia is a part of my name, that name starts feeling very unknown and strange to me. I have trouble accepting Samia to be my name. I really love the name, Sara. I feel very light and in my element as Sara. But the name Samia starts making me feel heavy. As if there is a deeply frustrating characteristic to being Samia. After two months of university, everyone starts calling me Samia instead of

Sara. I start feeling like a stranger to myself. I start having a lot less interest towards a lot of things. I somehow finish classes and come home immediately after. I always feel on edge at campus. I really wanted to be Sara, and run, and jump around, like a little girl. But under Samia's heavy, burdensome influence I can never be lighthearted Sara. There were a lot of things I was interested in, there were a lot of things I wanted to do, but all my excitement felt dulled by this identity. I hated being on campus after class. At home, where Ma and Dad called me Sara, I felt like I could let go and relax.

After many years of being Samia at school, I somehow finish my Masters. Some friends are looking for a job, others were already working part-time from before – experiencing life in a different way. Once I also really wanted to work, but by the end of my schooling as Samia, I felt like I had lost all interest in working. No one even wanted to have a romantic relationship with the girl named Samia, as if they were turned off by seeing her frustrated disposition. My family arranges a marriage for me. The boy lives abroad, he finished his PhD and is now working for a big company. I speak to the boy one afternoon on the roof of our building. He really likes my name, Sara, and calls me by the name many times as he talks about various topics. Doing everything on your own while living abroad is difficult. But now and then there are also opportunities to travel. Life is completely different abroad. I liked Abir from when I first met him. He is a wave of variation in my simple life. He makes me think about things differently. In my life abroad with him, I really like the idea of being Sara once again, but in a renewed way. At least in this new life, no one will be able to rename me Samia and take my Sara name away from me the way Professor Sara did. I once again live as Sara, in my own way. It's been sometime now since I've been living as Sara Abir Chowdhury in America's Dallas, Texas. I have completely disassociated and ended my time with the Samia name and identity. I took off the Samia name from all my identity documents, birth certificates to school diplomas. I replaced the name Samia with my father's last name instead. Abir told me I should just keep Samia as my middle name, but I told him I hated that name, he didn't say anything else on the matter. After getting married, I changed my name again to Sara Abir Chowdhury. I really like this name a lot. This is the name under which I got my passport, my immigration and came to America. Samia is laying somewhere in Bangladesh, dumbfounded that I didn't bring her to America with me. There's no mention of her on any identity documents. To make this happen I had to have a lot of patience and put in a lot of work running around from place to place. Trying to make this name change happen was a difficult task, people did not let it happen easily. In some instances, I had to pay people extra money just to do their job. In other instances, I wasn't able to get a hold of some people day after day. Others had endless questions, like why did I need to change my name, why couldn't I just keep the name I already had. Sometimes I didn't have much to say, other times I made up sad stories, so they wouldn't question my wants to rid myself of the dreaded Samia name. Telling a sad story works the best for getting things done. For example, saying that my friend named Samia committed suicide, or I've had a very unhappy married life, or developed some serious illness, thus changing my name may change my fate. People no longer ask questions when they hear those types of stories, and instead, just get the work done. I've had to go to a lot of offices and speak with a lot of people to get rid of the Samia name. Out of all those experiences, I've only come across one person, an elderly man, who just quickly did the work, without taking any extra money, needing extra time, asking any extra questions or causing any unneeded hassle. I've spent a lot of time living in America. I've adjusted to living alone now, doing housework, being on our own without other relatives or friends. In fact, I have far too much time on my hands, I'm not sure what to do with my time. Abir spends a lot of time with me after work. On the weekends we even go out to visit different places. Still, I have way too much time to myself. Abir tells me, "You should enrol in university here. If you get an American degree, you can get a good job. Even if you don't work, you'll still enjoy yourself, you'll learn a lot from going to school here". The thought of going to university triggers me to think of my traumatic experience with Professor Sara. But nothing bad will happen here, in a new place, so I agree to enrol. However, I give the condition that if I don't enjoy studying here, then I won't continue. Abir laughs and says, "there's no pressure, if you like it continue, if not, then just drop out". I apply and in a few months, I get in. On the first day of classes, the professor arrives for my first class. She's a beautiful, middle-aged woman, with blonde hair, blue eyes, a tall, slim figure and very pale, white skin. Despite being older, she has a sweet voice, like that of a teenage girl. She's very well-dressed. She lets us know that she's of Romanian and Greek origins.

After the Second World War, her grandparents left Europe to come to America. She was born in New Jersey. But she moved around to a lot of places in pursuit of her studies. After getting married, she continued to move around a lot with her husband, until they eventually settled in Dallas. Sadly, her husband passed away two years ago from cancer. She has two sons, one who lives in Australia and is married to a girl from Sydney. Her other son lives in Munich, Germany. He hasn't married and has no interest in doing so, he loves to travel around. So, our professor lives alone in a huge house, though not completely alone, her dog Jerry also lives with her. This is the first time in my life I've experienced a teacher speaking openly and in detail about their life and history. I've never experienced this back home. At the very end of her introduction speech, she says her name is Sarah Anderson. My heart begins beating faster, Sarah, again? Has another person once again come to push me back into being Samia? Why couldn't her name be something else? My eyes begin to tear up from frustration and anxiety. I decide right there and then, this is the end of my studies. Today's my first and last day of studies here in America. I won't come back to university again. I had drowned so far in my thoughts that I didn't notice when the professor was calling on me. "Young lady, what's your name?" she asks me. Everyone has been saying their names and it was my turn to do so. Startled, I go to stand up. Sarah

Anderson says, "you don't have to stand to speak, you can sit". All this time everyone has been sitting and speaking, I hadn't even noticed. Back home we always stand when we speak to the teacher. Sarah Anderson asks again, "any problem? Are you having a hard time understanding what I'm saying?".

She jokingly continues and says, "I've been here for so many years, but I still haven't been able to fully fix my speech. It's still influenced by all the people I grew up with in my childhood. And all the people in my household speak so many different languages. So, my speaking might not always be super clear to everyone. So please, if you don't understand anything I'm saying, don't be afraid to let me know". I didn't hear anything wrong with her speaking. In fact, she spoke very clearly and with great pronunciation. I was caught up in my own thoughts, so I didn't hear her. Yet instead of criticising me and looking at my mistakes, and saying things like, "if your mind is somewhere else rather than in class then you can leave", she put herself in the wrong rather than me. It's not right for me to allow a person with such a kind attitude to embarrass themselves. I try to loosen up a bit and smile and say, "your pronunciation is wonderful professor Sarah Anderson, I was really enjoying hearing you speak. That's why I got a bit lost in your words, and for that, I'm really sorry. The other thing is my name...", after saying that, I stop speaking. Sarah Anderson says, "thank you, thank you, so glad to hear that, still I know my speaking is not perfect, but what about your name?". "My name and your name are the same, my name is also Sara". I say this out loud somehow and then wait for her reaction. I close my eyes after saying this, afraid of what bomb she will set off after hearing that we have the same name. "Wow that's so cool, you have the same name as me, we're twins!", she replies excitedly. I look at her with my eyes wide open. What is this woman saying, "that's so cool, you have the same name as me". As if finding out that we have the same name somehow makes us closer, as if we're twins. Like how back home in Bangladesh, having the same name would make us friends – only if we're from the same social class and status. Or else having the same name becomes a huge issue of class discrimination. Yet here, this foreign woman, Professor Sarah, who is much more educated, older and of higher status than me, is accepting us to be the same, saying we're twins. What kind of behaviour is this? She doesn't feel bad at all that a brown girl in her class has the same name as her? Instead, she is happy about this matter, finding a girl with the same name as her. "Very nice to meet you Sara", she continues, and comes close to shake my hand. "Are there any other Sarahs in the class?", she asks. Everyone looks around the class to see if there are any other Sarahs. However, no one else steps up as Sarah. So we're the two Saras of this class. Sarah Anderson and Sara Chowdhury.

Sarah from Greece, Sara from Bangladesh. Mrs Sara, Ms Sarah. "I'll have a soft spot for Sara everyone, don't be jealous, after all we have the same name", says Sarah Anderson jokingly, letting out a sweet giggle. Everyone else in the class also laughs. "No, we won't be jealous" someone says out loud. After class, my mind feels very light and joyful. I feel very happy. Due to having an entire discussion about my name in class, many people already know me. Many people say, "Hi Sara", as they pass me in the halls. It feels really great to be known as Sara on this campus. I have no more thoughts left over about leaving university, dropping out or not returning. Discussing the first day of class at dinner with Abir becomes a nice and precious memory among the many memories of the married life we lived together.

Sherzod Artikov

Father's pigeons

"This is the place that you told," the driver said .

The taxi came to a halt near the edge of the road. I looked around from inside the car. The view – the edifice with two green cupolas and myriad pigeons around them appeared in front of me. Coming closer I found the yard full of pigeons which were eating birdseed scattered by people.

"Back in the day, it's called « Pigeon cemetery»," indicated the driver, following on me. "It's become the shrine of renowned holy man who lived in the city. The building at the corner used to be his praying room in the dim and distant past."

Plenty of people in front of that building were coming in and out turn by turn.

"Hundreds of people go on a pilgrimage every day," he carried on. "Here, people pray for the dead, patients for healing, childless couples for babies. They make imam* give the blessing and reciting the Koran** asking for invocation. Walking in the yard they strew seeds and make a pilgrimage to the holy men's grave."

I was keeping my eyes peeled for a flock of pigeons flying in the sky even I was listening to him, honestly. They were just the same as described in my father's album: bluish grey, white and black, more gentle and softer than each other as if giving meaningful look.

"Dear guest, I'll be in the car, "the driver said after some time getting prepared to get in. "If I didn't have an allergy to autumn air, I would escort you, unfortunately staying outside much makes me sneeze."

Blowing his nose, he walked towards his car. I came closer to the pigeons busy with pecking seeds. They were fighting over food as a few grains were left on the ground. In this case, the same as humans, the weaker group will be sidelined, luck is on only the more agile of their sides.

There was an old thin woman selling grains on one side of the shrine. I didn't see her at first. People were fetching grains in a cellophane bag from her. When I clapped my eyes at it, I bought some. Seeing me scatter seeds on the ground, I was surrounded by pigeons. Those flying in the sky also descended and joined the flock. In an instant, I was in amongst the countless pigeons. Forgetting fear, some of them were pecking my grain, as well as my hand, while others climbing up my shoes because of a squeeze.

Anon the bag in my hand was emptied. I sat down getting tired. There was a cemetery behind me. The shrine and cemetery were separated by a long wall, and it was clearly visible through the fenced chink in the midst of the brick walls. I guess there was a mosque next to it because the image of a crescent moon made of copper on a high dome was inclined to the eastward.

As I sat on the bench watching the pigeons, I took my camera and photographed them several times. Then opening my briefcase, I took father's album inside it. I compared the pigeons around me with the ones drawn in the album. I looked through the notes and dates written under the pictures there. Below each picture was a note and date. For example, next to the picture of a grey pigeon with the date « 04.06.1995 » was written « My darling, my child went to the first grade today. » Underneath was a picture of a white dove with the date « 02.11.2001 » written « Yesterday, I looked at the firmament through the window. I felt as if I was seeing you, Snow White. » Among them, the one that attracted the most attention was the picture of a black and white, plump pigeon. Father dated « 07.06.2006 » under it and noted down: « I bought chocolate from the store today, it has a picture of a dove on a package, just like you, Fluffy. »

When there was no one left in front of the scholar's praying room which had been mentioned by the driver before, I got up and went there. Inside, an imam with a turban on his head and a white beard was sitting in the room, the Koran and the worry beads were on a table covered with blue velvet in front of him.

"Come on, sir," said the imam, giving me a warm welcome

"I want you to recite the Koran for my father's spirit," I said when I saw his inquiring look.

He began to recite the Koran. Listening to him I visualised my father: I called to mind his last days at the oncology department of Northwestern Memorial Hospital in Chicago. Back then I often stayed with my father who was lying on the bed for the last few days of his life with brain cancer, lost his hair completely. He was emaciated and eyes were sunken. He always lay holding my hands, when I fed a spoon of water or soup to him, he looked at me smacking his lips and blinking eyes. He always wanted to say something, but couldn't speak as he became speechless, he was only wheezing.

One day, his condition worsened. As I didn't move away from him, I took the remote control of the TV set on the wall and changed channels to distract myself. At one point, father wheezed in a low voice putting up his right hand as if screaming. Pigeons were being shown on television. At first, I understood that his grunting was to change it to another channel. When I did this, he got nervous and his hands started to shake.

"Bring back the channel showing pigeons," mum approached father trying to quieten him.

After returning to that channel, father immediately calmed down watching pigeons. But his hands were still shaking, his trembling jaw seemed to be hanging if my mother wasn't holding it.

"Ramadan, did you miss your pigeons? "asked mum, gripping his jaw tightly to read his mind.

Tears welled up in my father's eyes, he tried to say something, but he didn't go beyond gasping for breath again.

"I think your father missed his pigeons," my mother said, turning her face to me. "In Marghilan, where we were born, there was a place called « Pigeon cemetery ». Your father's childhood was spent there. Even his youth. There were countless pigeons. Your father adored and passed much time with them. He took me there a lot, too. When we went, we always fed the pigeons sprinkling grains and sat dreaming for hours."

My father was lying quietly listening to my mother. One moment he was staring at her mouthing, the next at the pigeons on TV. Listening to her words, he more or less understood what she was saying, and perhaps that was why he wept bitterly and tried to get up wrinkling his border of the bed.

After finishing reciting, imam opened his hands in supplication. I also followed him.

"There's nothing wrong with asking," the imam said, glancing at me. "Son, you look like a foreigner."

"I'm from The United States," I said, introducing myself to him. "But I'm Uzbek. My parents were born there. They lived in Marghilan for some time and during the "reconstruction years"*** immigrated."

"They moved away before gaining independence, did they?" he asked.

The sky was dark and the clouds were floating in blue. The yellow leaves of a plane tree in front of the praying room were falling over the ground in the breeze. I reminisced about my childhood in Chicago stepping on the leaves. My father said that I wasn't born when they moved to the USA. Father had a deep affection for me as he was raised in an orphanage. Every weekend we used to go to either match of basketball team called "Chicago Bulls" or a nature museum. We also went to the cinema a lot. At night, I always passed into slumber listening stories and tales. Whenever he is free from work, he used to call me to his room and teach me Uzbek and how to play chess. At that time, he impressed me as a blithe and pleased person. On top this, he was very jokey.

Even after growing up, I didn't notice any common human feelings such as woe, longing or grief in him. True, sometimes when we came back on foot after watching the match of "Chicago Bulls" or drank tea on the porch in the summertime, his heart sank seeing a flock of birds in the sky. It would happen so quickly that he fell silent as if he had lost his tongue at that point where he was telling a joke or an interesting story, and sudden change in his soul continued for several days. Sometimes I saw my father opening the window wide and his eyes had a distant faraway look. Even then, the birds would be flying in the sky, my father watched their movements hearing their cries.

He worked for a diamond trading company. Even worked at home because of his busy schedule. Sometimes I watched him from the doorpost of his room and sympathized with seeing him working, wiping the sweat from his face. He worked over much, but in the meantime, he took a break and wrote on the album that I now have put his hand on his chin. Then I realized that he had drawn the pictures of pigeons at that time.

After his passing, I flipped through this album every night. Seeing the light in my room hadn't gone out yet, my mother often entered the room and watched the album together, her eyes filling with tears. The inscriptions and dates under each picture were more heartbreaking than the picture of pigeons there. The more I read them, the more I felt like I was bent over the flow of memories.

"I think your father wanted to go back to his homeland, "my mother said in such woebegone moments. "He wanted to see pigeons."

A light drizzle started to fall. October here is just like Chicago's, it's kind of cloudy and rainy. As it started to rain, the people who came to the shrine began to disperse. Seeing them go, pigeons seemed to be sad. They looked at each other as if they didn't understand anything and stared thoughtfully at the people's back who had sprinkled them with grains. Just then, the heavens opened and I walked to the car parked on the east side of the shrine to avoid catching a cold. The driver was dozing in the car waiting for me a lot. He woke up when I opened the door suddenly.

"Were you here?'' he said, rubbing his eyes.

On the way, it was pouring even more heavily. The car's windshield wiper was unable to wipe off the raindrops hitting it. Seeing the sheets of rain, I thought of the pigeons with concern. I thought they got caught in the rain. After a while, I reassured myself that there was a place for them to keep in. I couldn't stop myself thinking. Another thought, whether or not there would be a shelter for that countless pigeons began to flicker through my mind.

"Did you forget something there?'' the driver asked when I pleased him to turn back.

When I got back to the shrine, I got out of the car quickly. I hurried to the yard which had become a haven for pigeons. But there were no pigeons, neither on earth nor in the heavens, as if they had vanished somewhere without a trace. I stood in the rain for a while not knowing what to do.

"Did you forget something?"

The imam who was closing the door of the praying room gave the same question.

"Where did the pigeons go? " I asked, turning to him.

The imam looked around as if he did not understand.

"They went nowhere," he said in a calm voice. "Look at the roof. They have nests here."

I looked at the roof. At first, I didn't notice the shelter. After some time I saw a long, narrow passage. The passage was enclosed and there were several openings to allow light inside. The pigeons were closing up and watching the rain fall outside sticking their heads out from the windows.

"Do they all fit in there? "I said, looking at him for clarity even my concern had disappeared.

"Of course," he said, wiping his rain-soaked face with a handkerchief. "They have been living there as a family for many years."

When I returned to the hotel, my clothes were absolutely sopping. Seeing me enter through the main door, one of the servants there handed me a towel. While towelling, I ordered the manager a call for me to America. He immediately dialled the numbers I told and connected my mother.

"Mum," I said when my mother's familiar voice came from the receiver. "I went and saw my father's pigeons. They are the same as the pictures depicted in the album." Mother wanted to say something, but her voice didn't come out. Only the sound of her crying could be heard from the receiver...

Definition:
*Imam - a Muslim religious leader
*The Koran - the holy book of the Muslims
* Reconstruction years- years between 1988-1990 in the Soviet   Union.

Translated into English by Nigora Dedamirzayeva

Uday Shankar Durjay

For Cremation Ashes

Since last night, I've felt distress and unbearably lonely because my dog died of failing physical health; he had been suffering from type 1 diabetes for the last two years. He was on medication, but he could not respond to treatment for his declining health. I gave him a small dose of Vetsulin though it was not recommended by a vet. The recommendation was the full dose of Vetsulin which seemed to be extremely strong for him. He was with us for nearly five years and became more adorable as time went by. Basically, he was looked after by my nanny. I cried so much and still I weep and hide my face away from my partner. My partner doesn't want me to lament this loss. In his opinion I do care for my pet more than myself. It's perfectly true but really I can't manage to stop the tears. It's like I'm sinking in deep water.

Normally, as soon as I wake up, I go downstairs for freshwater. After having cold water I go to the washroom. But this morning is quite different. I find a brown envelope next to the door on the floor. That came through the letterbox yesterday for sure, however, why didn't I see it? I question myself. I remember I came home last night drunk and I straight went to my bed. Instead of going to the fridge for water I bent forward to pick up the envelope. Once I saw my name on it I couldn't make myself stop opening it. A lot of posts come with names of different addressees. I think those are previous owner's posts.

My nanny actually would look after him because I work full time and I'm so busy. I live alone, sometimes my partner comes to visit me. He normally lives in Newcastle and he is busy with his life. Considering the circumstances, I decided to keep my dog with my nanny. My nanny also needs a company, at least she can pass her leisure time with my dog. My nanny lives in Clacton-on-sea, it's just about a 1-hour drive from my home. When I was in secondary school I had a ginger kitten and she was adorable, sitting next to me all the time, touching me with her tail. She would sleep with me always. She would understand some words. I couldn't keep her with me as well. I was compelled to leave her because when she was growing up, she would try to scratch me and sometimes to bite. My mom didn't want to see her craziness which became more dangerous. Finally, one day the shopkeeper who would live in front of my house came and collected my kitten according to my mom's decision. I didn't get it back and my mom also didn't try to bring her back; my choice was totally brushed off. However, I would go to the shop, and I cried like a baby. I tried to control my raw emotions, but I failed every time. I failed to stop seeing her. As days passed my kitten became a cat and she started ignoring me. And after a few months, she won't recognise me, she won't show little interest in me.

I am an adult now, but my mind is still got stuck with those days, I can't erase the memory of 92 High Street. Still, I go to that shop and try to find out my cat, I know she is bigger now and all the memories about me have been erased. No one knows about her because a lot of cats in the shop around. Other staff at the shop look at my stupid face and might be thinking that I'm so foolish and animal sick. How freakish I take a peach to see my cat every time!

This is another dark morning for me when tragic consequences occur. It's just like the dusky sky growing behind me. Overcome by emotions I sit on the ground and weep. Why is it happening to me? What's wrong with me! Why does loneliness run beyond loneliness?

I don't want to kill my heart anymore. It's just a pin pricking in my heart. I take a deep breath, wipe my eyes and notice a half sheet of white paper on which a footprint is visible. I suddenly become quiet and speechless. An emptyness enwraps me. I am drowning in the deep dark. I try to touch his paw print, rub my fingers on it and I realise this is something that I lost forever. I can feel how stronger the bonding was. I can remember my mother, she left me when I was just two years old.

My nanny and grandad helped me to grow up with a lot of joys and happiness. However, mom is never replaceable. I pick up the brown envelope left beside me and keep my eyes focused on it for a while. I realised something inside the envelope which I missed earlier. I find that there is a small plastic bag and a letter together. Cremation ashes of my adorable dog! I can't stop my tears which rolls down from my cheek. I didn't expect this cloudy morning, even though I didn't think about it. My sausage dog died two days ago and I have received a small plastic bag which was full of ashes of him. I am getting out of everything. The broken sky falls down on my head and everything is inaudible to me.

I sit on the sofa in my living room and try to be normal. My heartbeat is high and uncontrollable. I have to get ready for my office and head out right now. I leave the envelope with ashes on the dining table, lock the main door. I make sure I take my car key. My car moves off and my mind is searching for something else like not other days. Today I need to keep this memory forever with me. After finishing my office I walk to Earnest Jones and buy a few key holders. I will use one of them and make it personalised by engraving such a unique message. It would be an invisible message which is just for me. It would be an astonishing symbol to carry on our beautiful time.

After such a long and pathetic day I'm exhausted. I'm ready to go back house. I'm not feeling well to drive for a long way. The choice is limited and I am just heading back my way. I'm driving fast like a foolish driver. My phone is ringing from an unknown number; I try to slow down and park my car at the nearest service station. By that time I have already missed the call. I call back and a voice comes from the fire station; the guy says, 'your house is on fire, still trying to control the flame to save but we are sorry'.

I can remember what I did before leaving home. I left the gas burner on because I was frying eggs for breakfast.

Part Five

Prose Poems

Poems by Daniela Andonovska-Trajkovska

Ontogenesis Of The Red

1. My Mother And The Red Sky

The red sky alighted on the lashes of the dream and saw it's reflection in the eyes of my mother who was looking for the story on her palms every night, the story that should have been born long time ago.

She visited physicians and fortune tellers and when she realized that she will not have me, she accepted it as a destiny and got rid of everything in the old house in which the ingrown nails were hurting the healthy tissue.

2. Me And The Red Sky

The first year, I was looking at the red sky for hours, and all the weeping stars were running down my face to teach me that everything that is up can come down and everything that is down wants to climb up in the sky.

The thoughts were stretching on the wrists to learn the alphabet of the silence.

There was a time when I could hear the sea in the shell and the music in the oscillating wire. There was a time when I could see the whole world in my mother's eyes and then I learned that the important things live in a dot and everything was born by that dot.

3.   Me And The Red

I learned the first letters when I was three years old, and I read "The Little Prince" when I was four, and I learned that taming process can open me toward another skies and I mustn't allow the child in me to fall asleep with theories and that my mother will be beside me all the time although I will try to escape from her planet many times in the future.

And whenever I went I returned home following the red.

4.   Me And The Exclamation Mark

When I was 16, my mother turned herself in a question mark, and I started to look like an exclamation mark.

- Where are you going? Who are you going with? Are you coming home by 12? Who else goes out that late in the night? Did you finish your homework?

- Out! With my friends! No! Everybody! No and I don't mean to do it!

I was writing in my diary with an alphabet that I invented with letters that were moving around and were breathing all by themselves. And I used so many so many exclamation marks, and all of them were addressed to my mother, because I was imagining her searching my drawer looking for a piece of my red sky.

And in my wildest nightmares, I was seeing her standing in front of me with the sky in her hands asking me where I had lost it or who took it from me? And how could I do such a thing and how could I allow that to happen?

I started to hate the red, although my sky was untouched.

5.   Me And The Open Sky

When the sky opened and looked at me with watery eyes, red poppies started to grow in my yard, and my soul was drawing circles from which the fire was dripping drop by drop.

And I felt, exactly in the same way like my mother 24 years ago; I felt hard kick on the inner side of my sky.

6.   Red In The Words

While I was drinking black coffee in my mother's yard, my son kicked the little coffee table that was heavy from the juicy cherries picked from the cherry tree that I used to climb up as a child and said that he dislikes the fact that my back is starting to look like a question mark.

- Put away your exclamation mark! – I told him sharply.

I bit my tongue, then, with the red words that reminded me that the time is round and that it crumbles red blood cells from its own sky each time. And the skies have similarities, at the end.

7.   Recognizing

The red poppies in the yard spit the sky in the center of the circle and colored the fibula that was recognizing its own sjuzhet lines slowly.

The two skies opened towards each other, and the red flowed in both directions without losing a drop of blood.

Translated by the author

Poems by Mostafa Tofayel Hossain

Beauty or commodity

Better is her presence here as a piece of values; or, preferable is her presence here as a piece of glamour; or, cherished is her physical aspects as a commodity of show; or three in one? How much one can exploit her when one is a piece of values? And when she is a piece of glamour? And when she is a commodity of show? Lotuses are worshipped; lotuses are set as symbols; lotuses are sold as commodities. Indira Gandhi was a paragon of beauty, but she was never a showcase; nor was she a saleable item; but she was valuable above par. What's in an object that survives time? It's not the look or glamour of the lotus as much as would make people get moved at, but the values of it in terms of her aggregate qualifications. None of the limbs of the dancer matters to time future; none of the music of the dancer that matters to time future. But it's the value of the dance she would leave behind her, well able to stir times durably that matters.

The new birth, the no birth

It was an achievement at the cost of a sea. A nation earned her rebirth in exchange for the loss of her entire erstwhile stock of blood that she had formed in her body politic. There was a proclamation; there was an oathtaking on a high mound of ground; there was a flag-hoisting signifying the rebirth, and there was a constitution to uphold each and every promise for the equitable share of wealth to be earned anytime anywhere anyway. It was a universally acknowledged dream, come true. But, all of a sudden the dream turned back to the dream; the fairytale turned back to the fairytale; the red blood ocean turned white coloured soyabean; and the ceremony of innocence of sacrifice turned to "A woman's story at a winter's fire,/ Authorised by her grandam." Yes, the new birth might have been a no birth. The resurrection was but a fresh visit to the underworld! And Jesus looked all astonishment, at Mary and Martha.

Bhasha Andolan

That was Bhasha Andolan. And, the Bangalees were looking for their identity in Bangla Bhasha, with a simultaneous venture to let others know that they're other people. But the others were well skilled in Columbusism or Clivism. Then the others opened fire on the Bangalees to confirm their otherness of language and philosophy. Those other ones once again crossed the seas and crossed the limit of savagery, to prove that they're more than the savages or less than the cannibals. So, the others got historically othered, leaving the Bangalees in the soil of Bangladesh to live happily forever, abiding by the principle of the oneness of brotherhood and equitable distribution of wealth among themselves. But the otherness again got cropped up stealthily! How strange in behaviour! How angelic in spirit to change their speed! How miraculous in adventurism learnt from Columbus and Clive! Now some of the brothers fly by Jets to America, while the rest of the brothers take recourse to small wooden boats in the Mediterranean, just to drown! Unity among the brothers was strength; can otherness among the brothers prove strength?

Let the Bangalees resume a Bhasha Andolan once again.

Poem by Chen Hsiu-chen

Organic Life

You spend your organic life. The first thing as opening your eyes, is going to slide your mobile phone, sliding to and fro, slide yourself into an unreal world. I spend my inorganic life. The first thing as opening my eyes, is going to see you sliding, your mobile phone, sliding to and fro, sliding me out of your organic world. In the farm of your organic world, are there cocks to wake up your mind? You spend your organic life. I spend my inorganic life. The first thing as opening your eyes, is going to slide your mobile phone, the first thing as opening my eyes, is going to see you sliding your mobile phone. Sliding to and fro, you slide yourself into an unreal world. Sliding to and fro, you slide me out of your organic world. In the farm of your organic world, are there cocks to wake up your mind?

Translated by Lee Kuei-shien

The Heartbeats

A clock was hung on the heartland of the living room, making a sound of heartbeats of an old house.
I was absent in your heartland, yet I desired to make the sound of your heartbeats. You occupied my heart land, but made a sound of others. The Son of Man was hung

on the heartland of history, making a sound of the heartbeat of the rebirth.

Translated by Lee Kuei-shien

Owls

I am secluded in a mountainside domicile, watching Taipei 101 building through the opening window. At the bottom of a tall bamboo joint, an owl hid there. Like all owls in the wilderness, at night stare its round eyes, like a pair of diamonds. Owls have a full body camouflage, except for the high-resolution eyes by neglect. In the dark night, I conceal my black eyes due to insomnia, for the basic need of security. I am something like a quiet hunter, but as soon as confronting to a owl with strong challenging eyes, I become as if, a voluntary sacrifice

Translated by Lee Kuei-shien

Poems by Pran G Basak

Criteria

The mysterious intention to go and think again and again the purpose. The next step is to put the guidelines on the schedules. In the heavy blue sky above my head, I saw cruel blow one after another. I call the flying birds and say, brother, be careful, everyone. Take the wind with you, don't believe the flight if the weather isn't properly right. The shadows are on our feet, we talk, there is a slight change in the routine during rest and hence the friendship. Friends today have gone to the city flat for an unavoidable reason, obsessed with the future. When he returns, he is sure that there will be no more sunshine on his wings. As I go, I wonder who I will tell Infinite Infinity. As far as the eye can see, it is not out of bounds. And what the mind sees is not infinite, it revolves around it. And from so close to each other, it seems that you are infinitely far away.

River n d sky

While wandering through a path...or...a desert...searched for a river with utmost Eagerness! Beside d nearby thorn bush Or beside d heaped sand-tilla....! Asked about a river..to an more inclining shadow of an inclining old tree...got no answer! After a short silence...it made a hiss sound Like his conical shade.,And uttered 'Don't know driver! How is it?.. But yes...somedays ago before twilight a folk singer passed through my shadow... Was singing with tears..n uttered he was also searching for a river since countless years!..and told me...d enormous stars of d sky And d stylish moon only knows D whereabouts of driver! Since then I was watching d sky But noticed only poisonous blue spread And poisoned blue spoiled body!

Translated by Bani Chakravorty

Inside eyes

Kept everything secret inside you got down on a wide spot ..Which was loaded with ample sunshine! At d end.. got a continuous veranda..with some light n shade! Dialogue begins behind d screen. Silence talked so much .. N.The fields cultivate words n words. Your paramour takes an oil bath in a pond behind and collected words collected Alphabets....instigate bubbles while sinking inside! Takes one dip... Three dips..five dips to calculate a sum..while wet clothes increased his glamour. You weave dreams with warm rice. Nostalgic scene of college life comes on d way..u think how many countries are there...countries over country! Unknown country... He lives there.. wrapped with ice with beautiful landscape! A sign on cheek which got from a sweet Dream of dawn...washed away easily ... But d eye inside d eyes...can see far.,.. Far...behind d eye-sight can reach!

Translated by Bani Chakravorty

Poems by Umapada Kar

Untiled

The words of intense affliction may rest aside keep apart the erased afternoon whisperings. Please come to share the fresh pleasure of the morning, just now, before the sun becomes thickened reddish. Sleeping bedstead has not kept words, nor the pillow too. Still, I am fresh after a sleepless night. This is with an anticipation to complete my bath with a little jocund-water. Report of your sleep may be beyond my knowledge. I don't know, how much dense were the curtains of window to prevent light from outside, or how much influenced you were being wrapped by the zeal of quilt. Loo king you fresh also, that's enough. Who are those to mix the sound of morning flute with air? Let's think that is for ours, friends with sugarless tea hope that we shall be glad, sloth air holds the sugar-pot in hand, if it needs a little. The morning is waiting only for us from the dawn. Please come, let's enter, and exchange our places. Let's share the amassed melancholy which is part of pleasure as bonded by wedding.

Untitled

Chameleon pulls its hand back after touching lightly. Warp of sari is in metamorphoses colour weaving out flying butterfly, nothing can be better than this.

Windows of the closed room are opened after a long period, but sunshine is scarce today. Dampish, few moist frog's croaking are entering the room. This is also a special gift like rainbow. Some kites are flying in the sky at their heart's content, the horizon is giving cordial reception to their behavior like whirling, curved dipping, and ups and down. Globe is rounding on its own imagined spine aside, and within this periphery we the small perpendiculars stand erect. Anxiety is noticed in all, useless laugh, only butterflies and kites are flying away on saris and in the sky. These are allotment for us to release the skin of concern.

Untitled

The mind becomes delighted by few drops of aroma. I am scattering myself the whole day and night. Flash of delight on the face of public. Bowing their heads, the mob is passing away calling me an extraordinary constantly. I don't know anything about this. I was walking simply in the middle of them, even not laughing, a fright made me puppet from the beginning. Then, why all of them are so pleased and why they bend their heads from shoulders. All they are reading me thoroughly, targeted me minutely. And they have seen certainly such a thing within me so that I have no alternative but to startled. I am enjoying this utmost, though sweating internally.

Translated by Author

Poems by Shikdar Mohammed Kibriah,

Calling Indian Cuckoo

Enjoying our teletalk by full moon and lively sky. On that lovely night, I said: "Look up at the sky". You said, "What a wonderful moon!" I laughed and said, " This is my friend's face!" You laughed too and said, "How much love! What a fancy!" " Not a fancy my dear. It's your true analogy. Elusive!" I'm not an astronaut, Neil Armstrong or likewise. I've neither any spaceship nor knowledge of technology! I merely heard the popular song of the Bangla cinema "Sujansakhi" ---"Don't raise your hand to the moon while you are a dwarf"! Tell me how I could try to touch the moon! At my touch, she'd be slurred. Scandal will explode on social media. The famous song of Shah Abdul Karim that I heard: "I'm an unchaste outcast! Don't let anyone touch me." Or that song of a saint from Badarpur "If my wind touches somebody, he will lose prestige, property etc. and be felt severely"! But how to keep off the wind thinking that whole the night all of the mango buds fell in the stormy wind and the Indian Cuckoo called non-stop dawn to dusk:" What a woe I have!" "What a woe I have!"

Postmodern Democracy on Non-Stop Bus

Democracy! It's modern. So outdated. Now it's the postmodern age. Let's be a little bit postmodern. Western democracy has remained modern. Not a few changing at all. Neither Canada nor Uganda. How can be the role model of postmodern democracy? Let's have a look at the third world. Excellent uninterrupted democracy stirring up in the People's Republic of Bangladesh! Could be a role model of democracy? Absolutely alike our old model town bus. Passengers get in and down nonstop. Have a look at a different scenario. Running public bus. Nonstop service. Unlocked closed door. Waiting two passengers on the sideway. Female! Quick eyeshot catches two empty seats still. A sudden break in non-stoppage. Stumbled nonstop bodies. What happened! Why stopped! Cried all loudly. "What's late in just two minutes. Look women here!" an audible humble voice from the driver. But isn't it a nonstop service? So what! Motherly women standing in the sun! No lacking of supporters. Humanity is the first. How the blind supporters say-Development is the first, next to democracy! The busy helper gets active- move! move, please! go back. Haven't we mother-sister! Wow! Great humanist! Again, stopped in non-stoppage. It's Traffic Week. Papers checking. Highway police browbeats the driver - Take it out! Hurry up! The driver pushes the paper —Yes it's paper! Move! The bus moves on non-stop. Sounds simple. And democracy speedily runs to achieve a magical postmodern goal.

Fashion Profile

Wearing velvet pants and a blouse-tight shirt easily went into two huge ears of a rabbit and became a young man at the age of thirteen! Private cars on the city way already changed their turtle model to be looked handsome. Their humble figure is now nose erect. Sweet fragrant surroundings. Pink scented dress. French perfume. Covered the world with huge black sunglass. Blazing pop man with High-heeled shoes, big watch and long hair covered the ears. Just for a decade. Pages of history became yellow. Putting on loose shirts in skin-tight pants I'm a disco dancer. Rejected Dilip Cut. Shaved both sides of the head. Followed Jackson and now Ronaldo style with a designed beard. Every temporal man wants to be changed in fashion style. Changing days, changing fashion but man remains merely a man.

Poems by Alok Biswas

Locked in Darkness

always feeling aloof, roaming aloof... though some candles in between... make us forget to be aloof, but we don't bother... the candles transform into landscapes, transform into fairies, into golden paddy fields not to mesmerise, but to be something else, perhaps thrilling pibroch... they pass through our veins rendering otherly sensations...but we look down to the distressed river, the river not in fact bloody at all, rather filled up with eternal water... we kiss each other, sexcise each other, but know not why feel traumatic... we try to tear off the dark feelings, dark feelings soon start revelling before eyes... so to escape we again kiss more stirringly with futuristic interpretations, but all goes in vain... our vision turns blacker and sobber and we fall into a cave embracing each other supernaturally...

The Crushed Folk

a naked with coordinating nakeds in power... people are not laughing but crying as they find nothing to cook for their children... the budding flowers to have breathing problem in smog... the naked howls with other regimented nakeds... while baking our measure bread, it seems the breads don't get baked... the children remain unfed, the pets remain skeletoned... the plants seem to be changing into desperation... the nakeds have stored caravans of wine bottles and cakes... now found dancing in weltered rains singing for more powers coordinating with tyrant nakeds... a missing link intervenes to set ourselves apart from raising any voice of protest...

Improbable Destiny

keeping a purse is not difficult... one may not agree, others call it a bird, as it sometimes disappears... one keeps it in the subconscious and whenever he likes, it comes up to his desired premises... the question of it being lost improbable as the person concerned ever remains mingled in it... the purse lost means the existence lost... the man hides his existence... he never allows it getting lost... the purse may be seen floating far off or flying with some butterflies or lies hidden in a Nazi gas chamber... yet it's never lost as the owner of it always stays sleepless in the purse... but in a crucial phase he knows not how he reaches the destiny holding his spouse's hand who to has always been in the purse acting as an ultrasonographic director...

Poems by Joanna Svensson

The Autumn Light

I sat in my hammock – watching the pale sunset. I just sat there in my hammock – feeling a beginning of stiffness. It felt somewhat chilly and then I did notice that my whole appearance was covered in a thin white sheet of newly fallen snow. I had not noticed that fall had passed. It felt just like all the clocks in the whole wide world had stopped. Made halt. Forgotten their function. Broken their springs. Already when it still was summer. The clockmaker of time – I met him early one morning. His voice was filled with sadness when he told me that he just had to stop the time. For the one that I love – most of all in this whole wide world. The one I loved most of all – had just gone, passed away, started her journey towards the light, moving to the other side of the rain. My dearest mother who gave me life – who gave me courage – who gave me wisdom. The clockmaker asked me quite specifically. Not to be sad and not to be afraid. -It was your mother who told me to stop the time because she felt that her own time was due. So even if you missed it all. All the colours on the altar of fall. Do carry safely in your heart so young, the knowledge that it was your mother who told me to stop the time for her so she could go on towards the eternal light! -So when you start the time again, now with her soul in your heart. 'Cause, she will always be there for you within you to guide for always! For a moment I froze in my current position. But then I strongly felt that my mother's words, interpreted by the clockmaker of time, had given me the strength to brush off the snow from my clothes and take a big step into the future!

The Gentle Veil of Midnight

I sit in my amber-coloured library with my weary head deep resting in an old leather-bound book with family photos. The burning of the midnight-oil had ended long ago. The gentle veil of midnight sweeps my mind as well as my thoughts and gives me comfort. For no one sees my tears. The steady wings of time seem to lift me towards the sky and I feel so light – almost weight-less – and so filled with power and inner strength. And I allow myself to cry beneath this gentle veil of midnight. For the tears do clean my soul – wash away all negative vibes. Brings balance to the present and in what has just passed by. Now all bad thoughts will slowly fade. Just like a forgotten painting. Like a watercolour in the rain. The tears will wash the troubled picture away. In the end, all colours will just evaporate. All lines will vanish and what's passed will dissolve in the purifying tears of rain. So, when the new dawn will rise, then the future will hand me his palette with brand new colour tubes, brand new brushes and water-colour paper. With this in hand, I can start painting my own new picture of the future!

Actually At The Moment, Really

Today I have put everything on hold I have actually
paused all of my thoughts, all of my dreams and all of
my wishes and longings. Everything I really want to do
– actually. Because at this moment the whole Universe
holds its breath in total shock and watches what's
happened recently. With sad and frightened eyes it sees
and reflects upon what the world is actually becoming.
So actually, in order to be able to look myself in my face
again, I have to put on my colourful and enchanted coat
and go for a long and self- contemplating walk. I take
the opportunity to greet the springtime that comes
around this time of year, every year – no matter what the
inhabitants of the earth contribute – actually. So, at the
moment I have put everything on hold. Have actually
paused all of my thoughts and dreams, wishes and
longings. All of this in order to survive – actually!

Poems by Saubhik De Sarkar

A Mild Red Line

A bird took a flight towards the tattered spring. Stones rolled down following the marks of failure. You remembered the lead roles walked towards the river at the end of an implausible film. You remembered after an unbelievable murder-scene you choked thinking about your mother! Before believing these falling apart scenes in the dead afternoon rays you felt that a similar scene is being re-enacted. Within the spells, our sharp whistling you story's hero walked till the trench!

Heavy war-wind on one side of the trench and in your circle
History of subalterns burning side by side a provocation

Twenty-seventh March

Shirt fluttered slightly and we witnessed the crime through the clouds. The moon glided by this time. People conceal very familiar desires in their hearts, crosses a station to observe a dead friend's house. Nonetheless, our houses are accumulating in a wrong ship's story. We're talking about sexuality, the clouds swinging behind it! How the mystic ballad crosses the undefined field approaching us! Nights are flying away hooting down the cold moon. Our botched journey, humiliation and the seasonal Saree escaping through the frightening trees! The firm belief, in reality, is, in recent times standing unbuttoned is one's writing stark opposite to the eclipse. Squandered marks of travel before a fabricated fight. Stirred up provocation concealed by talons and claws. In reality, all these are mistakes of that unseen exodus! Father Varghese's blue bicycle got up before shedding sin and grief-stricken swimming baptised us evading the fresh, raw hair of my girlfriend.

Preparation-phase

The sky is condensing again after its stillness. Preparation-phase! As if the earth was awaiting this moment. Your Mother burnt! Blank mortal body! After repentance, the unaware feet burnt at a distance, burnt beliefs, a few flights like the ancient signs. In this universe today, sunshine is spreading like a wrong dream. We yawned below the cheeky clouds. Upside-down noon tilted carrying the seeds of remorse. Your hand trembled before touching the iron keys. Thinking about an unbelievable night Linen sheet shivered. A yellow dragonfly flew towards us crossing this infinite noon, from faraway against winds incomprehensible songs played on radio at the rail-lascars' taints.

Translated from Bengali by Dolonchampa Chakraborty

Poems by Hussein Habasch

A Traveler

I

As his puzzled legs like, he travels. He crosses long distances and dangerous bridges with no doubt that he will make it even over his dead body. From springs, he drinks; in deep rivers, he swims. He suckles fresh milk from the breasts of she-wolves: "Thank you, fierce mothers," he says. Under a plane tree, he rests, and with a provocative desire, he contemplates the cracks in the valleys. After a scared rabbit, he runs, and calms her with a carrot that emerges from his heart like an arrow. He wallows in grass and mimics the birds in the sky. He jests with the squirrels, tossing them hazelnut; here and there, he joins their jumps. He waters a flower and in return, receives a whiff of perfume as he whispers to her: "He who has flowers, has no need for God.". When he feels hungry, he knocks on doors like a passerby, asking for bread to share with his siblings, the birds. He falls in love with the first woman he meets, as if she's been his woman for a millennium; he leaves a kiss on her forehead. He does not care when his heart is worn out of love or vice, and he says to it: "Thank you, my big heart!". Near a sparkling spring water, he lies down into a sleep of all nightmares. He opens his eyes to the sudden appearance of a lioness nearby. In a cold manner, he says to her: "Claw's morning, lioness!" He asks indifferently: "Do you prey on dreadful poets?". The lioness turns her face and runs away from him. He tightens his backpack, and off he goes toward oddity, with no burden of a home, a homeland, a woman or a child. Wherever he stops at and fills the place with the water of temptation, he calls it homeland. Wherever he takes the earth as a bed and gets drunk on the damp grass, he calls it home. Each woman he comes across in his travels, he calls his own. A sparrow, a butterfly or a star... let his child be. Here he is standing on a highland, getting his act together and kicking the butt of sorrow. As intense as his own death, he shouts: "Oh life, I will devour you! Where to run?".

II

He left no sea without slating his body with, nor a mountain without giving it a pat on the head. No forest, unless he obtained it out of its arcane; no land, unless he planted it with his madness. No language, unless he learned its most impudent vocabulary, most hurtful and evil. He passes through each and every border; "Thank you, my strong legs," he says. He finds himself everywhere, "thank you, my wanderer soul that roams the world.". In the huts of the poor, he lived; he became one of them. Into the palace of the rich, he entered; he could not stand it. He knew hotels, bars and sidewalks the same way he knew his parents, siblings and friends. To homelessness, the same way as to his torn socks... He drank, got drunk, smoked. With indiscretion, with delirium, he filled the world. He loved trees more than human beings, birds more than planes, autumn more than the other seasons. He loved the night, he grasped his hand and told him: "You blind man, how much you enlighten the hearts of poets.".". He knew the cold and wrapped himself in it. He tested the strong accent of the snow, he cared not for it! He did not take storms in earnest; his face kept butting against the forehead of the wind. As he dies in the grave where he lies, there will be no ease; from one grave to another, one graveyard to another... He comes across the ancient dead men; hears the bones rattling across the fresh dead to hear them decay. Across those who were sentenced to death, to bliss, and those who are swinging on the Straight Path. The one eternal traveler he is; one doesn't dare to ask: why do you not rest? God shall judge him, yet "What has the insanely sad one done to be judged", the traveler shall ask. "Why did you create me after the image of the mad and not after the pure image of yours?". He attacked frustration, but it penetrated him with a bullet that was not stray. He hit the roads until they were worn out, the soles of his feet cracked, one by one, the toes fell apart. "It's all right, travelling is prettier.". In his entire life, he had no money; scraps were enough for him. On the edge of an abyss, his life was. On the sharp edge of existence, his heart was. With stubbornness, he kept telling life: "Be generous with me, o life! With growing intensity, be generous with me; for I love you with all of my passion and immense generosity."

III

As a guest at the garden of the blind, he came so close, staring at their eyes, beaming with blindness. All of a sudden, he remembered J. L. Borges, "If I could live again my life,... I'll try to make more mistakes.". He remembered the blind man of Ma`arat al-Nu`man, healing pain with forgiveness, forgiving no one. He remembered José Saramago leading the blind all over the city, killing and wreaking havoc... He remembered the lover of Jun'ichirō Tanizaki, piercing his eyes to be as blind as his beloved. He remembered the old blind man of his village reciting from the book of God and gathering the angels around, and how, he himself, was gathering all the devils around old blind men. Now, he opens his heart, totally blind... from the abyssal depths of his blindness, he beams with ecstasy.

IV

Rain is tapping against the pane of his heart. He sticks his head out and says: You rain, hit it here on my head, exactly on the carefully polished skull. I want the rotten mind and his resident farce to be driven away! Under the strong, your strong stings; I want the salt of wisdom and the pus of certitude to dissolve. I want the rock of quietude to crumble, the throne of the taboos to collapse. I want to keep the madness glittering, beaming, enchanting, bizarre and out of norm. I want the beings to breathe sharply in amazement and
repeat: "How majestic is this enormous mad traveler!".

Translated by Azad Akkash

Poems by Masudar Rahman

Wooden gun

Wooden gun - carrying have been long for years, should finalise with you today or tomorrow. Maroon gemstone in ring finger - got the gift from you on our amicable days, its touches have grown leaves and buds on the gun-butt. A whistling bird sat on the look-alike 'pointing index finger' rigid gun-barrel

Easy

Light is lenient, cannot get in if you shut down windows. The wind is simple, so it tries to go easy straight ways and fall apart onto the complex. At dawn, birds wake up in the bamboo forest, start gossiping on these topics about the light and about the wind, in an intense and tumultuous manner. I took off my shirt and stood at the easy light. Watch me, see how complicated I am! The wind is blowing and my wearing green lungi is getting swollen like a balloon. It's dawn, sunlight is approaching. Rabindranath is as decent as light

Journey by Bicycle

When getting out for Bicycling, the topic of the Moon
obviously comes upfront. The profound evening.
Musical dark starts spreading. The Paddy field. Paddy
fields covered the horizon ... zigzag; muddy roads are its
flat palm-lines. As I'm out for bicycling, my dog is
following me. The round food-plate moon shining over
the evening sky. The bicycle running. My dog is
following me back. Sister Ranu's pet moon is
accompanying on our way home.

All of them were translated by Ashoke Kar

Poems by Sumana Ray

Nobody Nowhere for Us

We idled away our times in projecting bridges by
flouting river in moonlit gossip. One or two aimless
grasshoppers are floating over our blue-painted tapestry.
While fleeting by our side, the diminishing full moon
announces the advent of enveloping darkness. We sense
our words get sluggish. Many words get lost before they
let loose from our minds. Tumultuous river drives away
Mendel's law and his metaphor-ridden pages from our
drooping life. We hardly exist anywhere as we dispatch
our eyes around—a life sans history.

Moment of Truth

Jilted clouds are descending from missing boatman's
ominous bulletin. From Fida Hossain's brushes dissipate
sprinkled darkness in the gleeful canvas. Loathing
confluence of clouds and earth impregnates light wind.
Carefree words deserted by rains unleash a strain of
melancholy in the grey land. Birds are voiceless. The
sky fades far away in the broken halo of hopes. Amid
epidemic's invasive darkness, we are alive in the many
faces of death; each breathing epiphanizes moment of
truth.

The Night and the Moon

As we ponder over Foucault and Freud, we pass old post-box. Lampposts are then busy figuring out their last night's geometrical intricacies. We bear witnesses to young hearth dissolving in rusty wind. The sky, laden with medley of clouds and rains, is wandering iterant o'er our heads. We carry burden of memories along with dreadful hours. Our hoarded wreckage string of mud drains out in river in want of care. Our arguments to dissolve. Hush! the moon and the night woo in the body of river.

All of them were translated from Bangla by Dr Nitai Saha

Poems by Quamrul Bahar Arif

Stay Up if You Wish—

You stay up like my beloved on art-words stay up in the crevices of the reddened bricks of Somapura. The stair that rose from Paharpur goes up…There I will revel in the intense thrill of listening to the sound of your footsteps. At the peak of Adinath or Rankut there's been no last stair at any time; only enlightened spirits. They climb up, only up in the sacred shower of light… You stay up, in the waves of mothering green. I will open my eyes and see how much light you have gathered in your sailing boat? How much love is in the native tongue of eyes? What an overflow of love? You stay up if you wish—in these inebriated, endless eyes.

Translated by Ahsan Habib

Daughters Pilgrimage at a Sacred Tomb

Jumping the stairs of some aforesaid tales she, my daughter crossing the way of her expected pilgrimage tales are reaped by her ages of eighteen, enlarged from few to enormous in her mind, so no tiredness nor the weariness decays or defeats her long passing. Stepping one by one she going near and nearer to her blessings of dreams. I guess the wings of tales are spreading within her, tales are lying like a green, green field with endless crops reflecting on the deep deep green horizon of the village abroad. Her stepping is alike the linkage of the river, stepping became an era to an enlarged era. My daughter gets wet by the softened fresh air of river Modhumoti. Thus, she becomes the aged of several eighteens, all the tales, all the dreams within her emerge with the turnings of her voyages. Accessing the stairs, all the way, at last, she entered with an idol of year and era in her soul. She entered at her pilgrimage, she entered at that sacred tomb of Tungipara. At that very moment, all the tales all the dreams within her became an epic, a holy book. I with her in immense tranquillity, with her worshipping, raised my hands and looking the holy cover of the epic, hangs on her face, on her forehead. I was overwhelmed, I found the enlightened name of Shaikh Mujibur Rahman.

Translated by Bithi Mazida

Man or Devi...

Let's assume you are a woman who just came back home after her worship, or you are a Devi, you attained completeness, let's suppose your river-water and wind, too...You just bathed in beauty—at the behest of lips and eyes, in love. Your beautiful body is filled with spiritual purity. You walk in the pure, floral fragrance of rebirth. With the steps of faith in the breaths of the wind waves... Let's assume I am dissolved in your lips, eyes, in the sacred beauty of your body. Then I can take it I am within you, a man or a Devi...

Translated by Ahsan Habib

Poems by Antje Stehn

Ephemera, the Mayfly

A stair step counter like me meets Herman Hesse
everywhere the calf is slaughtered within twelve months
the daffodil picked and withered hanging over the edge
of the vase, after a few days the outdated selfie of a
childhood friend that makes you wonder when did he
loose his shiny eyes

On my screen a stranded insect fragile delicate
transparent wings in the dark network of veins stares at
me with glossy eyes for him only one day to practice life
I carry him gently
to the open window.

Pegeon Dinosaurs

The flourishing dynasties evicted from their attics find
refuge in wired basements of tenement houses as an
impoverished nobility. Some try to regain the freedom of
flight fluttering excitedly   around the sharp spikes of
social deterrents a ball of slate blue plumagepecks at my
windowpane watching me like a curious tourist lost
outside the entrance of a stately home the red eyes full of
determination and pride of lineage as masters of the air
for generations and I watch with reverence the dance of
the bonsai dinosaur on my windowsill.

Coloured Sweater

Today the colors of my sweater remind me of those tangled threads that electricians eviscerate from the bowels of the street. Today I want to go outdoors walk barefoot beneath those creepy glass towers curved like dripping glaciers. I want to hear the memory of footsteps rising from the asphalt become a part of that foggy coat covering the earth right below covering the fertile soil between the trolley tracks where slender blades of grassgrow.

Poems by Prottoy Hamid

The Shared Blood

When you kiss her, you kiss me unknowingly. Even when you think of kissing her, adoring her, I feel the urge in me! And every touch you make to love her, or to rule, I sense it. But the sense does not say how you are now, or what you think of the weather. Do the clouds full of cold rains snatch you out? Does the green still make you crazy? Whose eyes do you look and dip deep into? With all the treasures of love we shared, your touch from every inch is flying to the sky, or to the hill-top where our words of togetherness are still mixed with all leaves and drops! They have never heard of your friend who lived in Canada and has returned with many reasons for you. Coins have that sound you could hear easily without knowing that the sound of love can only be heard with the heart. How you are, then, I always wish to know, and how our shared blood, our princess who could not sleep without our kiss, my kiss, is!

The Cry

People are crying. Oh, relax, I have mistakenly used the word 'crying'. People are laughing, but it sounds like crying. Again, I have made a mistake. People are laughing, but it seems to me they are crying. Sorry, it's a mistake again. People are not crying. They are trying to cover some untold pain: the pain of which you know, the pain of which he and she know, the pain of which we all know! It is I who translated it as crying. I need to be hanged, they say, but my tears will preserve humanity some DAY...

A Passage to Golden Crops

My journey never ends. The Sun always tries to overpower me. In return, I always send smiles to him at the end. Every day I start earlier than he does, but we stop together. I have to. I want to save daylight. This saves my land. Moon comes sometimes to see me. We sit together hand in hand and gossip. I share the day. I share all that I do from dawn to dusk. I share all about my conversation with the green plants and grass and the soil. She always loves the one with birds and butterflies. But I have less time to talk to them. Sometimes when Sun sends colourful light in the evening, and the birds and butterflies dance around, I leap and talk and sing with joy. But I keep going. I never stop. My steps always move forward and explore new soil where my hands sow seeds of "Mercy, Pity, Peace and Love". My journey never ends. Even night my veins run towards the dream- the dream of waking up on a fine morning and seeing the whole land full of golden crops.

Poems by Mariia Starosta

Reflections of a Woman

I Have Dreams

I have dreams very similar to reality, but they have no vile deeds and losses ... I have dreams with your messages, in which you wish a good day or morning, without a doubt and a flower to remember. My dreams end with the first sight of my eyes, but warm impressions remain. I live all day as if you actually greeted me in reality. You don't know: someday I will send you a coloured gif from my reality. You, I know, will think I'm too confident, but I don't care. I want to read your messages, even if I'm not modest, even when you disappear from my dreams for no reason, but I will believe ...

Western Sun

Western sun, you have crossed half the world and shone with your rays all those who needed light and warmth, who wandered in search of truth and who have already seen everything and are reaping the fruits of their life experience. Western sun, you will return tomorrow with new hopes for a new day. Western sun, your golden radiance ignited not only dreams, but kindled with fire in the depths of the soul, so that each day was not lived in vain, but became a continuation of the blessed life given by the Lord.

You Remember

The morning smells of flowers, the sky smiles through the gloomy clouds, a new day of new hopes and impressions is revealed, when a delicate flower has sunk into the soul…You remember…

Poems by Mili Roy

Lamps of Hope

When our solitary times strike their heads against a wall of numb sensations, the unfulfilled words of countless shattered dreams come crashing down on the alleys of our minds. Who desired to be tethered to the thread of existence yet ended up getting lost in the never-ending river of time. Like a crookedly streaming river, they seek to discover their existence at every turn of life. But eventually, get lost, being unable to find the desired destination

Hundreds of words, hundreds of life tales have been buried in the dreary emptiness of an exhausting time. Fragments of hopes have been scattered about carelessly and negligently along the path. Dreams perished while fluttering their wings in our everyday restricted existence, with their gaunt aspect. They couldn't reflect the words of fine craftsmanship in red and blue patterns. The mountains of frozen thoughts did not melt at the threshold of joy. The dreamer's soul often wishes to drift away in a handful of sunshine. It wishes to sweep away the lamps of desires in the creases of clouds. I wish to attach myself to such wild ideas. Captive aspirations and ambitions, on the other hand, find fulfilment in the midst of thousands of emptiness, in unfathomable perfection, and unconditional exceptional expectancy in the hands of fate.

Twin-Flame

You were hidden like a stream of diamond in a rain-showered wave inside my head, at the threshold of self-realization. You built yourself as classical music builds itself up, by the letters of the rain calligraphy, and the collage of the sun, appearing as another form of myself. The designation of my desired life was inscribed in elegant jewels. The four-dimensional light reflected on your face like a pleasant graceful soft slit, and the flute of Chaurasia chimed in the seventh melody of poem and light. The aroma of austere living enchanted the Royal Poinciana, dawn brushed up against the big smile of the horizon. The forsaken breeze of Mayurakshi river returned to the entrenched resonance of the sprouting leaves. Poetry is instantaneous, only when the watermark merges with the hues of life. Even in the unconscious darkness of Vidarbha, I could feel my soul's affinity to this face, which is as gorgeous as the sparkling raindrops, the connection of thousands of years of birth and rebirth. Droplets of grief were collapsing because of the endless amount of bliss! During the most challenging phase of life, girls mature into becoming women, in the twilight of time, in the wonderous period of a growing cane vine, in a spellbinding way.

Two-Dimentional Era

In between the calling of the new creation and the fall of yellow leaves, lies a bohemian period. On one side, the brave ascent of the young leaves, and on the other, the bare retreat of the old leaves as they fall. The world of dazzling emotionless light is on one side, while on the other is the stagnant time lost in emptiness. I wish to touch this nameless interval in between the erosion and reconstruction of nature. The falling leaves are well-aware of the agony that the Purvi raag is enduring while being played. There is a remarkable gap between the bright light of a beautiful afternoon, and the timid light that is devoted to darkness. Meanwhile, the day's cheetah burns by the wrath of Deepak raag after all the hues of the afternoon have faded. The world cried in primitive lamentation. On the opposite half of the horizon, the stars merge, in the silvery light of quiet. I want to reach out and touch this enigmatic two-dimensional time in the midst. What is this tune of Chaitra that I'm hearing, on the precipice of life and death?

Poems by Anindita Mitra

When Rain Joins

When rain joins the swollen river in spring, all catches for discomfort are smashed, yellowish strange leaves begin to shiver, the light of *kojagari* full moon floods the body, two sets of lips get closer on the lonely beach, exists only endless dreams fuelling fantasies about fulfilling intense desire. With immense sorrow, your shadowy figure gets mixed up with mine, tears drip silently. Discoloured alphabet hidden in my bosom takes a tumble at your Cherrydown East house, fallen feathers dab sunset orange tinged with cinders. You start to laugh, read a work of fiction secreted in my mind.

Translated by Gauranga Mohanta

Twilight

The last orange colour sunrise at dusk came to your verandah. Gray crows were kissing each other. The leaves of the Jill tree were swaying in their way. The sorrows crossed the boundaries of happiness of the exciting spring days. Your fingers held the weight of my memory, I cried in hidden those days. No one was next to me, so I wanted to give up all the pain to the sky. There is the colour of mourning, its own colour. Soundless waves make light on in front of my mind.

Death wants to swim in my hair sometimes. I don't question.

Translated by Nurjahan Rahman

Memories of Silence

All the light of youth has fallen. An open forest of loneliness on the top of a bare hill. Silent memories come differently, the moon has got black clouds, The pungent smell of gunpowder on the bloody highway, vision got faded through. Intense smoke. I become speechless being burnt in the fire of mourning. The canvas is captured with the random depiction of a thousand words. The melancholy rumble of violin, the material of the city of Paris, the unique shadow of the sound of rain in the lonely chest of solitude. Sometimes, words want to be wordless.

Translated by Nurjahan Rahman

Poems by Mahfuza Ananya

I'm Washing Away My Hands

I'm washing away my hands from life so that I can deny, deny the generation, the time and the blazing fire within clotted blood. I have kneaded time like bread, made the dough and ate as if it tests like burnt meat. I'm washing lumps of time away from the mirage of history and phrases. When civilization is dying, the golden flies of confusion has been overcasting everything. I am as helpless as the motherland, I have no head, no pillows under my head! And literacy-heroism has been sleeping like a corpse. Or suppose I'm a small river, how can I hold its over-flooded banks? The palmist is counting my misfortunes, has deciphered exciting opportunities into the garbage, into the dead crows gut, did find sighs of the century inside the madman's lungs. What would I do with such a small life, the vultures, the lion-kings are relaxing into the bloodstream; I'm washing away my hands from life, cleansing my clothes.

Yellow Punjabi

Miscellaneous seasons are entering into the life, Jesus of lustrous hunger, have you been to notice the yellow Punjabi clad spring? The southern wind entering into the room Oh dear love, are you still alive? Why aren't you coming inside me, the way poems get into green retina! For the yellow Punjabi, being infinite growths of emptiness into a two-inch brain! How much illness can it increase? Oh, my love, Language didn't learn you or innocence didn't learn you, you had constructed a quadrangle of seventeenth at the base of seven! Into heart-related intra-atomic smokes, you've blown out the symbolic orgasms of past days and my melancholy spring is learning native homosexuality...

A Letter Composed in Eighty-three Words

The orphan child if someone asks her name she can't even clearly express it, 'Bangladesh'... Bangladesh is an orphan child who has lost herself, no one knows her address? She only weeps day and night over, even if someone wipes her tears, she can't provide the address! Two pathetic hands of this country are spreaded toward the sky, lips recites prayer. Even though nothing can't satisfy any pity. Losing all her dignity she is now like an old lady, her shrunken breasts are hanging hopelessly downward ...Bangladesh has lost her destination and now weeping by the side of an unknown pathway. She is so thirsty that is quenching the thirst with her own tears ...

All of them were translated by Ashoke Kar

Poems by Aliza Khatun

Lost Watch

Beyond the faraway deserted twilight the movements of the watch had just squatted. In the depressed fuzzy darkness. After the desperate search for the watch, finding it nowhere I dispatched some of my very intimate moments to Arunbari, Behula, Mohipur, Shrirampur even in all the villages of the world which belong to me and us.

The time escaping from the orderly cage of the watch and ran with tremendous speed towards these villages. Innumerable fearless and dedicated well-wishers Were diligently trying to find out the watch. Whereas I was drown in the prayers and wishing, the watch might be lost forever. All the moments scattered in miniscule particles on the bank of the river full of harvest in the polite heights of the bamboo bushes nearby the almost extinct tradition. Every moment which I had dispatched, returned back one by one with variety of self-charming golden sights.

At the Dying Place

The disobedient windows of morning yearns- for annoyance. They want silent sunlight, slumber afternoon, and the twists and turns of the path. The tired birds are hanging on the branches- of cripple-dream-tree and the definite afternoon evaporates like camphor. In every day's press briefing innumerable ceased heart beats are shown- in the fluctuating charts. Like a pendulum, the habits of passing time swings on the wall of hope and despair.

Under the dominance of N95 mask all expressions of the isolated heart even the desire to get you know intimately suffocates and dies. The talkative evenings evaporate in the thin air from the steaming teacup. The moments pass away, and the life goes on besides the lightning struck moments resides the momentary evenings the dreamy time disintegrates from the integrated map and the gravedigger's soil remains dumbfounded. Being soaked in the alkali of soda and soap the charming faces are becoming vague- like old, engraved letters still hope persists – in the persistent blowing wind, there will be clear diluted message "Please comeback" although there is very little hope.

A Strip of Sunlight

There were still some sleepleft in the eyes of the dawn while opening the window I saw – the book I was reading last night still lying wide open. A strip of sunlight fell upon the black words of the opened pages, the warmth and the sunrays made the alphabets alive the words and sentences became active one after another, every chapter like the hamlets of habitats indifferent from the color of darkness became clear and more intense and turned into ebony black.

As the day grows the body of words become intense bright and sharp. The dark black bodies made of coal, glittering embers here and there. They are standing in queues covering white sheet and becoming harder and harder by burning in the severe heat of discrimination. The suffocation of Floyd. The reverberation of that painful suffocating breaths, glued to their chests, the protests go on and go on and climbed down from the white pages to the busy highways.

All of them translated by Haikal Hashmi

I'm Trying!

Since last April, I have been trying, Camellia, to turn you to ashes in my heart. There you have been just more burning fire. I'm trying to close my eyes so that I don't see your light; yet my eyes, open or closed, end up not being able to see the light of any women other than you. I'm trying to avoid all the paths to you; yet I see myself nowhere other than on the paths to you. I'm trying to head towards a direction opposite to yours; I don't know what power drags my legs toward you. I'm trying to dispose all of my memories with you into the well of forgetfulness; unwillingly, I see them lightening in my memory. I'm trying not to utter your name at all; I see it only glistening on my tongue. But I will make you a promise: I will forget you! No, no, no... I'm not making any promises to you... I'm not making any promises to you. Goodbye for now... I miss hugging you so much!

Translated by Azad Akkash

Poems by Sutanuka Mondal

The Question of Existence

Ordinarily they visit the place alone; no one cares, no one questions. The dried flowers on the ground that lay; feasibly, submit the question, "But on what I lay?" On a deceased body or a man of intelligence.

The familiar companies visit alone, new visitors; half-experienced they say. They have never sipped the potion of life- Wine, Poetry, Virtue and Pain. The dried flowers laying on the ground questions, "Where's the parity of existence then?"

And if sometimes, on the steps of graveyards, or in the solitude room where one mourns for the dead; the dried flowers lay suing the winds to wave. Their groaning and moaning turns into a murmur. A murmur of which the visitors hardly care. The rolling of life-pebbles revitalizes its desires. "Are we martyred?", they again questioned.

Half-experienced visitors now giggle and say- "it's time for you to drink the potion of life. Choose between the Wine, Poetry, Virtue or Pain".

Clinched Flowers

As gently the winds brush their petals, they sway in tenderness cuddling the nudge, pleasure of a moment or two, seizing the day. Hitherto, their freshness will fade, reducing to silence at the end. The selfsame swain will then slip by scrubbing the dwindled flowers.

Anthophiles too abase them, shrinking to mere dust. At most, a seller sells potpourri, a miracle whole. These flowers moko-ed a memo, beyond the meadow of our soul. Our lives and after lives meander into diverse lines; little does we know.

Amidst Silence

The night, deep-dark and sable, is the perfect time to weave a fable. The hand glides on the paper with fervently burning eyes. Drowned in passion, penmen allow their feelings to dance. Their feelings dance on the white canvas with Euphoria, Happiness, Joy and Bliss recurring on their yarn.

Phantasms of hope sometimes repeal them. The forlorn past knocks their head repeatedly. And, with wet-eyes, a weeping-heart penman keeps on penning Misery, Agony and Sorrow. Reflecting upon the trauma of a troubled soul.

They yearn to pen down pleasant words. Thus far, their heart fails to work. Trying to not invite sorrow, verse-makers hunt disguise of happiness. Turning memories to a vague lane of a storm cloud day.

Even so, amidst silence, a faint image of agony still bides. Barely resisting the harrowing memories to fade.

Poems by Mridha Alauddin

Homeless

Your bare body, well-shaped rich breast, soft and puffy cheek and the perfume of musk on your hair. Didn't let me sleep at night. Fire is in my whole body, and I'm overwhelmed with passion. I have been homeless to get home.

Translated by Sayeed Abubakar

The Wandering Bird

The splendour and unique bird was confused and was only saying. Love you, love you and love you much... And one day the bird with the nomenclature of love adorned with a soft tiara flew away wearing a vivid and colourful silky dew drop dress. The bird went toward the south on a dark night where evergreen leaves lay on the ground. The bird was getting restless, erratic and disoriented in her flight. After wandering the river, vast blue sky and unknown world, the bewildered bird returned to the green horizon.

Translated by Tuwa Noor

Verses for The Perfect World

In a brilliant and miraculous hanger. In a hanging porch or an equivalent sea, or in a deep blue sea, I'll purify today's submerged civilization. Like the drop of saline water which is a symbol of health and wisdom. The grenade-attached world will be purified. The cleansing against capitalism and imperialism

Astonishingly, this is the way to educate the sightless eagle on how to speak. The purification is for the flowering in the dark and haunted land.

Translated by Tuwa Noor

Poems by Hrishikesh Goswami

Rain And Humanity

Every dawn it rains but every morning is quite unalike from the previous. We constantly slip out something in the long run, which is now dubbed as Humanity. I miss both of them. Rain teaches us to pierce even into the slenderest of the pores while Humanity makes us Human! Who is fearless enough to ace the smidgeon cries of long-lost Humanity. Let us all get self-possessed and cry out loud in the label of Humanity and Rain.

Upside Down

How self-seeking these hominids are. They love to see their turnover everywhere…no matter where they are! And for this, they are set to do no matter what. They can make you feel low by sighting matter which actually is bogus about you. And when all these happen you feel irate, miserable and disheartened towards that particular soul! YOU somehow forget *yourself* and stab to find cues that will sanction you to chasten that corporeal; and if you are not able to find any, you will again come up with collusions and avowals which actually are not true for that person and all to compensate for your lost prestige. And the worst part, this cycle runs till eternity!

Genesis And Repercussion

What has caused it to rain? You say it's evaporation! What has caused it to evaporate? You say its precipitation! Does that mean a ring has no starting or ending? If it is like that, then how did its manufacturer begin? I might be joking but that is not the case! Genesis leads to repercussion and repercussion, in turn, causes genesis! Respect is born out of a decent result and virtuous respect holds your esteem high. But if you want to keep that respect live, you will have to learn to respect. Respect even that dust grain beneath your boots. I might sound a bit impractical but that's not the case again!

Part Six

Letters

Letters by Nivedita Lakhera

Letter One

Dear one in love,

I am so very happy for you.

Your blessings are our unmeasured value. Love is
Heavenly because it frees the limits our known
existence imposes. You are where life can transcend
through physical flesh and greet the soul directly, an
experience like living in a temple of innocence,
Where your faith in the beauty of life is restored.

Where even though all the doors of all yours senses
are open, for some reason only magic enters to worship
the heart.

While all of us are born with the power to love, a
tew lose our courage to do so till we are rescued by
the playfulness of transient time and another
glorious soul.
May a thousand words shine on your heart so each
heartbeat becomes a song, and may it be so scared
that it becomes a prayer of love, for all the gods.

So hold on to the one you love.

The one who makes your mornings more peaceful,

the one who stays with you like a dance of life, the
one that is your rock, the one who both challenges
you and comforts you, The one who helps you grow,
but also rejoices in who you are.

There can be many destinations, many roads, many
travels, but you will only need one home.

Enjoy this experience of the height level. I hope it
lasts a lifetime.

Remember, you see as much beauty as there is love
in your heart.

So be in love and stay there.

Namasate

Letter Two

Dear Majestic Warrior,

The undying twinkle in your eyes will always shine
Your road ahead.

It's your little visions that will make a light to fight the
darkness in the most humble yet powerful ways.

For there will always be a path that your soul will
Carve through mountains of impossible, and that
My darling, will lead to the greatest adventure that

Your heart seeks and life celebrates.

Because the best part of getting lost is finding an
Unexpected journey and discovering an even more
Amazing version of yourself.

Like a shooting star, traverse your sky and unleash
Your glow, I promise, the glimpse of you will fight
The darkness for at least one soul that needs it the
Most.

Keep burning, keep shining, let the light flow.

Remember, you will always be more than the noise
Around you, and taller than the ceiling of
Resistance. Remember to be you, and remember you
Are all those things and much, much more.

Along this journey, a few wars will be given to you to
Conquer the self. Those are the battles worth
Fighting.

Let the fire that burns you become an eternal light
For all.

I am so proud of you, remain glorious.

Namaste

Part Seven

Reviews

the wear of my face by Lizz Murphy

Reviewed by Penelope Layland

Picking up a new volume of Lizz Murphy's poetry always involves the added treat of imagining the unfamiliar words being delivered, straight to one's innermost ear, by Murphy's distinctive, wry, Irish lilt. As an accomplished performer of her own work at Canberra-region poetry events over many years, Murphy's audible 'voice' is, in a fashion, inseparable from her work on the page, and so it is with this latest volume, *the wear of my face*—though perhaps this new work penetrates the ear with a little less lilt and a slightly heavier heart than hitherto.

Arguably, it could not be otherwise. While some of these poems have been a decade in the making, they have been brought together in the smart of bushfire smoke, published during a pandemic and sent out (via a Zoom book launch) into a world in which acts of terror and inhumanity are only ever a news bulletin away. The mood of our times unsettled, distractible—permeates this collection. Readers familiar with Murphy's work (she has published eight previous books of poetry) will find many of these new poems more fractured and fragmentary in form, and perhaps less conventionally narrative, than some of her previous work. There is a sense here of a poetic intelligence looking sidelong, as one looks to the night sky to see objects of distant beauty—even when the subject of the poet's focus is something concretely calamitous. So in a poem about the busy workday exodus from suburbia, with its 'magpie eisteddfod' and 'cockatoo saw', we are left, finally, with a woman, behind a 'peaceful façade', 'alone with her healing her dread the boozie / smash-mouth nightfall'.

Murphy's eye for a truthful, pungent image is as strong as ever, and her gentle humour thankfully survives these strange times. So we have 'prickly pear like thorny mittened hands', and the backs of an old woman's knees as 'miniature lilac landscapes', a brown goshawk 'skirring overhead, wrists pushed forward', the poet smelling 'the iron on that man's / shirt', or the taxi driver, pausing in his work to lay his prayer rug in the taxi rank, his place of worship delineated by 'the sycamore's embroidered bark / its shimmering lime canopy'.

The matters that have concerned Murphy poetically in the past persist in this collection—especially social justice and the lives of women: girls, vulnerable to predation, but also older women, or poorer women, or women displaced. Murphy's interest in finding poetic inspiration in found texts and visual art is again apparent, and the collection includes an arresting ekphrastic series responding to photographs of refugee children by photojournalist Magnus Wennman. There are also a number of reflective poems in the collection that touch, tangentially, upon the health system, poems set in waiting rooms, or on the road to and from appointments, or in carparks—the liminal spaces where individuality is strangely set aside, but where poetry may be found.

POL (Poetry Out Loud), issue 03, published in 2021

Reviewed by Saleha Chowdhury

POL means Poetry Out Loud. Or I would say Pot of Literature. In front of me is a yearly POL magazine. It is colourful and big. Lots of articles and poems to read. This one is issue 03, published in 2021. The main editor is Uday Shankar Durjay. Yes, I know this hard-working gentleman for a long time.

When I see the editor is Durjay, I feel proud of him. He is a huge thirst for literature, he does some fine literary works too. Writes poems, essays, short stories, published books and helps an Ancient Mariner entitled Saleha Chowdhury. (I guess he helps others too).

I have received POL, 3rd issue. It has essays, poems, book reviews, interviews and all. He does the painstaking job of editing, printing, distributing, and collecting raw materials for it and others. Now the question could be -how does he manage to do all of those? I say it is possible. Now I remember an anecdote on the issue - 'How a writer finds time'. Once in Germany, one ordinary man asked an Author -'I wonder how can you make so much time to produce all those books? I don't get any time to write a letter even.'

The author (I forgot his name now. Was he Thomas Man, Gunter Grass, Hermann Hess, Herta Muller or someone else?) replied -'Look the difference between readers and writers is just one thing and that is - in all our duties and jobs in everyday life we can make time for writing or you can say literary works but you the non-writers couldn't. Or I say we can put aside time for doing books and words. But you never manage to do that. Please remember this is the only difference between readers and writers. Between you and me. And no other'.

Yes, Durjay can put aside time for his fond subject the literature. He loves to quence his thirst for poems and others. Thanks to God! This sort of people makes us joyful and thoughtful too. The theme of this special POL is prose poetry. I remember he told me to contribute. But I forgot. Or I was having a hangover from that illness which nearly killed me. Now I see the rich harvest. His search for prose poetry results and I am astonished.

I get enlightened by the three articles on prose poetry. Lots of information about it which come in handy when we need them. Three essayists on this subject are - Eva Aronna - A Brief History of Prose Poetry. And the second article was written by Shikder Mohammed Kibriah and his article entitled - Philosophic discourse of Prose Poetry and the third article was written by Rashed Uzzaman and his article named -Origin and Development of Bangla prose poetry. I read all three and enjoyed reading them. Who would have known in Bengali prose poetry Bankim Babu's contribution? It's worth reading for our eternal thirst for knowing something new.

Those articles are in this Anthology and it's in part one. Then we see part two. Here we see poetry with poet's notes. Five poet's contributions are here. Then comes part three I see each poet has written five poems and the total number of poets is twelve. And in part four - I see four poets have written four poems each. In part five each poet has written three poems. The total number of poets in part five is thirty-one. In part, six three poets contributed two poems each. Please get the calculator and count those all up. Durjay in his editorial says - 'The POL always wants to put as many poets as possible. In order to share their individual thoughts and flavour of each other's poems. POL has created a platform for poets who are willingly exchanging their imagination throughout the world. 'So this book has a global identity and tries to collect thoughts from all over the world. Why not? The Earth is just a planet.

I wonder about some of the words I read used in translation! But the original is not here so we can just hope it's the proper translation. But we know something is always lost in translations and they say that something is a poem. But I am not so sure. Once William Radice told me something new about lost in translation bit - 'Suppose you got some gold in a riverbank mingled with the sand. Then to separate the gold from the sand you sieve it. Eventually, you realized the sands were gone and just the gold in the sieve. I say the same in translation. The dust goes the real essence remains.' I think this is a positive way of looking at the translation. As I believe essence is the most important element of the poems and I hope each poem in POL got essence intact.

Some of the poems I read in POL are playing in my mind. Like Relationship by Quazi Johirul Islam. It's sweet and I know now he has written 22 books of poems. I would request him -'please keep writing poems. It has a global beauty.'On page 160 I see Sidharta Sankar's poem, Munch. This is one of my favourite artwork. His poem about it is funny and enjoyable.

On page 134, Amita Bhatcharrya says - 'The reason I create art and poetry is that I must. It's a must. It's the only place every single inch of my soul finds a distilled and sacred place to unfold.'It's a good enough reason for writing poems. Like John Fowels I say 'When we write we write basically to realise who we are'. As we know 'The soul searching is essential for us.' And man does not live by bread alone. I hope the man includes a woman too. On page 113, Durjay in his poem is talking about a special vision. The poet has a third eye. 'I catch the same rain and no one read my mind. It's dark like my eyesight. All the crestfallen threatened to overwhelm me.'

What Lipi Nasrin is saying in a 'Spring Evening' -'They fall suddenly saying nothing. It leaves a mild ripple in the air. Its skeleton breaks by the thrash of storm remain like the fossil for eternity holding the memories of the time.' Here I love the word music.(page 183) I can give lots of quotations like that but I better stop here and request -'please get a copy and read. You will have a handful of gold'. The Book Review of Gauranga Mohanta is excellent. I must say it's a scholarly work.

His collection of forty poems translated into English entitled 'A Green Dove in Silence'.Dr. Nitai Saha has written this review and it's great to work with. I know Gauranga Mohanta through Facebook and I met him in Dhaka. One quote is like that 'Escaping the ruthless eyesight of the bullets we stealthily made an onward journey in the deep dark paths of the village. As we desired to come back, catfishes proliferated in our ponds, the courtyard would be covered with bean's verdant tenderness' A nice quote I see. Though I have not read the main book but hope to do so in future. Sometimes book review does that to readers. We feel desperate to have the book and Nitai Saha's words on this are like an invitation not to be ignored. And we wait to enter Mohanto's world.

The interview of Wali Mahmud by Farids Yasmin Tithi is another good one. I read it and love it. We may or may not agree with Wali Mahmud's every word but no harm in reading and it's a good read. Well-chosen questions and appropriate answers. This magazine is not Durjay's man's band. Others are there too, to make it a success like David Lee Morgan, Ashok Kar, Louise Whyburd, Daniel Sanchez, Joseph Imhong Cho, Abbie Neale, and Gauranga Mohanta. I wish Durjay well and my blessings with him always.

The Art of Hearing Heartbeats by Jan-Philipp Sendker

Reviewed by Louise Whyburd

A beautifully written book by Jan-Philipp Sendker. An endearing read from start to finish telling the journey of a young blind man and his journey navigating through the world. This is a tale that will draw you in from the beginning. The unfolding love story and bond between father-daughter that underlies the story throughout will have you completely immersed. A heart-warming story that will have you smiling through to tears with its delightfully written words. The tenderness of the author's words and description of the world that surrounds the main character through-out his journey makes the book a fabulous all round book. A five-star read.

Printed in Great Britain
by Amazon